C000054837

FOR YOU

MIKE MCCRARY

FOR YOU

MIKE McCRARY

Very few of us are what we seem. - Agatha
Christie

PART ONE

ONE
TONIGHT

WHAT HAPPENS after he kills for her?

After tonight, will she truly see him for the first time?

This and many other questions blitz Zach Winter's mind.

She said she was sad. He heard her say that with his own ears. Heard her say something about sadness at the coffee place this morning. Hannah was there with her sister, and her sister said she wanted Hannah to be happy.

Their conversation vibrated the core of him.

Her exact words escape him. They've become mangled noise, a twisting hum fading into the back of his head. Zach had been too dialed in on Hannah's face to soak in the specifics. Too wrapped up in the life and light in her eyes to hold on to the details of what she said. But what her words meant—what she was saying underneath it all—that was clear as crystal.

The very thought of her sadness hurts him.

Thinking of her this morning makes his heart skip a row of beats. She touched his arm at the coffee place. A first. As if she knew things were escalating between them. Zach read online that's how you can tell if a woman is truly interested in you. *Into you. Cares about you.* However you want to say it. Yes, sure, the look they give you and the words they use are important, but those can be drenched in mixed signals and cloud the true intent of what is behind those amazing eyes. But if a woman touches your arm, that's an unmistakable sign.

Was Hannah giving me a signal?

She couldn't bring herself to say the words. Of course not. Not a chance a woman like Hannah Rush would come out and tell the guy who works at the coffee shop how she feels. Zach gets it. She'd never be so obvious. So clumsy or so common about it. She'd leave clues. Breadcrumbs leading down a path to her. The sister saw it too. Her eyes watched Zach closely. She's a good sister. He hears Hannah talking about her sister's daughter all the time. Hannah's precious little niece. She's probably great with kids. Be an amazing mom, no question in Zach's mind.

Connect the dots, man.

It's what's between the words. It's the in-betweens that can save us. Or slaughter us.

Zach stands in a yard outside a sprawling home. His clothes are covered in random splotches of a deep, rich red. Almost black under the light of the moon. A spray of crimson is streaked across his face. The remains of what he's done.

Red and blue lights swirl around him.

So lost in his own head, he almost forgot he's holding a gun. Part of him thinks it's funny he never even used it inside the house. So worried about the sound. Now, he's holding his gun to the head of an internet-perfect woman he dragged outside. Angling her, using her as a human shield. No doubt the social media darling had a much different evening in mind when she showed up at this house to party.

Police are screaming at him. Guns raised, ready to remove him from the planet.

Zach doesn't hear a word they say.

The night air is crisp. Not cold, but it has enough bite to get one's attention when the wind picks it up a notch. There's a freshness to the air as it blows through the flowers and trees. Zach turns his head slightly, looking down the street at a neighborhood that's been gentrified all to hell. Young money coupled with aging hipsters mixed in with people pouring in from California and New York have turned this once *bad part of town* into what many consider a cool place to drop a million or two on a home.

Zach feels that tickle he's become so familiar with over the last year or so. The one that starts at the back of his skull. The place where the spine and mind collide. Then the hum will begin, one he can feel in his gums. It creates a buzzing he can't quiet or dull no matter what he does. He's tried. Talking. Pills. More talking and more pills. Got himself a meditation app. Said it was free; it wasn't.

An overweight cop screams for Zach to let her go.

Zach's family tried to help him best they could. Which is to say they were no help at all. He considered reaching out to them before tonight. Played it out in his head, visualized the conversation that would more than likely take place. A conversation that would end lacking in every way.

It's easier this way.

Zach can't hold back the creeping, clawing fingers pulling at his mind. This man's house. So many women. So many soft voices coming from bodies made of soft skin that wanted that man.

He gets it. Tall, with a flawless jawline and a slight English accent he turns off and on. Zach overheard one of the women say something complimentary about the man's eyes. This man— this Gareth—had a few bucks in the bank, plus spending a lot of his time at the gym.

What's not to want.

Zach's been following this perfect Gareth for days. Well, days and nights is more accurate. Ever since he saw Gareth with his Hannah.

How could Gareth do this to her?

She thinks they're in love. Completely unaware he's the one fueling that sadness she told her sister about. She doesn't know the kind of life this man leads, what he does when Hannah is not around. Rolls over women as if they were speed bumps. She doesn't know about the parties he throws at this East Austin bachelor paradise. Tonight there was a gorgeous mix of perfect humans. People who have everything all of the time. But not one of them can come close to Hannah.

Another cop holds his open, plump palm out

flat, his other hand placed strategically on the gun at his side. He's asking for Zach to be calm. *Odd way to go about it,* Zach thinks. More police vehicles scream into the neighborhood. An SUV skids to a stop across the street.

There were moments in the house where Zach's sight went white. As if he went out of body. His brain shut down while his body did unspeakable things. He had worked through what he'd do tonight so many times in his mind.

He was coached by the best.

Connect the dots.

They told me she would never listen to me. Some girls need to be shown.

Still, he feels he needs to talk to Hannah.

Sure, they talk almost every day about all kinds of things, this and that, but never about anything real. The time has come for real. Stop this pathetic shit. Stop this standing out in the night air armed to the teeth like a crazy person. He'll watch Hannah as she connects the dots for herself. A light will glow and grow in her amazing eyes as he explains. She'll smile that smile that breaks Zach in half almost every day.

There's a muted giggle from inside the house.

Or was it the wind?

A dog barks in the distance.

He's sweating, didn't even realize it. Zach rubs his eyes quick. Can't lose focus. Feels like his mind is floating more than usual. He squeezes his eyes closed, then opens them wild and wide.

From the SUV, a man and a woman step out. They hold badges out for him to see, as if he didn't know they were cops. Zach hears the man say they are detectives but can't make out much more. The man is older. Big. Towering. Dressed like a slob. Zach imagines he played football in high school. The woman, only slightly shorter, wears a sharp business suit and has eyes that cut through Zach.

It's what's between the words. It's the in-betweens that can save us. Or slaughter us.

Most of the beautiful people ran away from the party once Zach flashed the blade. Not so cool when things get scary. Zach had the idea to grab one of them. Keep one. This one. This woman he now holds at gunpoint in the front yard.

He adjusts his grip on the gun.

The woman's entire body shakes as he forces her to step back with him, arm around her throat, pressing the barrel to the side of her head. There's an alley tucked away about a block over. This woman has an Audi parked there. He saw her park and then walk over to the house. Watched through the windows as she placed her purse in the kitchen near the door he used to enter the house. He has to move quick. Not sure if the police have covered the entire area yet, but they will soon.

The detectives move away from the SUV begging for his attention. Other cops still hold their aim on him. Time is running out. Blinks. Mind skips. *How did he even get here? To this place in his life.* He works at a coffee shop. A single name punches a hole into his thoughts.

"Hannah," Zach calls out.

The detectives pause, look to one another.

"Hannah Rush." Louder. Harder.

The night air pulls tight. Zach's heart pounds.

"Hannah!" Screaming now. Hot tears roll down his blood-sprayed face. Then, as if a string was pulled, he slams into a chilling calm.

Spine stiffens. Eyes blank and cold.

"I did this for you."

TWO
EARLIER THIS MORNING

"SHIT."

Hannah Rush checks the time, then pockets her phone.

She's late. Of course. Always late. Her sister will give her that look when she gets to the coffee place. Drinks last night caused her to tap snooze for the third and fourth time this morning. She'd had to Irish goodbye the dude at the bar last night. At least she left before she drank enough to wake up next to him. Liked to think those sorts of mornings were past her. Love to think there's some growth beyond all that, but growing ain't always in a straight line.

She shudders at the thought of it. Envisions the verbal, perhaps physical, push out the door. There would be the all too familiar Hannah head-shaking, self-assessment moment once she was finally alone. Asking herself why she had to have that last drink that turned her judgement to vapor.

Thankfully, last night was not that.

Last night was an office happy hour—double the reason to tighten things up—not the land of blurry-eyed giggles and hookups. She's done the soulless apps and the setups from well-meaning friends that have gone a different direction from last night. Neither right nor wrong. As long as she's in control of the outcome, she's cool with all the growth. No matter the emotional bumps and social bruises.

Own your baggage, she was told once. *One of the few things in life that's completely yours.*

The guy last night was nice enough. Somewhat cute, in the right light. In IT, or some blah-blah job genre, but he fired off this clingy, needy sort of vibe. She could tell he wanted more of her than she was giving. Meaning, he seemed like he was seeking a girlfriend—whatever that means—then he'd want that wife for life, in addition to an evening of easy sex. Wanted to plant his flag so to speak. Speed up the process of endless suburban days by nailing pretty, damaged Hannah. The divorced woman in client development.

The one who likes to drink. Likes to party, as they say.

She knows what they say about her. Most of it bullshit. Some of it true, but still not fun stuff to hear. Nice Guy Computer Genius probably thought he could fix her. Mend her battered wings.

He'd droned on about his brother and his two kids. How cool his brother's wife is. How his super-cool sister-in-law juggled it all. A big-time pharma gig, two kids, and still worked out like a beast—his words. Which is fine, nothing wrong with it. Plenty of ladies on this rock who'd be cool with that version of life. But he won't be rolling with pretty, damaged Hannah Rush.

Besides, she's been seeing someone.

Nothing crazy-serious or anything, but Hannah would rather not screw things up with Gareth before they really get started. At least give the relationship a chance to find its legs and roam wild. Hannah and Gareth did meet on one of those soulless apps, sure, but it had gone differently than she expected.

They hadn't ended up in a drunken, fleshy pile. Her choice. And he seemed cool with it or at least acted like it. She has no illusions of who he is. A British accent attached to those abs doesn't come around every day and more than likely he doesn't have to wait for many women, if any. But pretty, damaged Hannah is trying to do better than the low bar set by what *many women* would do.

Her phone buzzes.

"Shit."

Her sister, Corny—Courtney actually, but Hannah changed it years ago—is texting her again. No need to read the message. Hannah rounds the corner. Downtown Austin already has the scent of barbeque and tacos. Never gets old, even at a pre-coffee seven in the morning.

Pushing open the door, she immediately sees Corny in the back corner. Hannah holds up her hand, avoiding eye contact while nodding her off. A fruitless attempt to defuse what's behind the look her sister is firing at her.

Corny smiles back. Hannah can see her annoyance melting, as she gently holds something in her hands. Hannah squints, trying to focus in. Looks like a square, paper something. Must be something her niece made for her. Hannah's heart flutters. Loves it when little Luna makes her things.

Hannah thumbs toward the front counter. Corny holds up a cup of coffee—*she's good.*

Moving up in line, Hannah spots her favorite barista. Her buddy. She comes here almost every morning, one of the few constants in her life.

"Hey, Hannah," Zach says.

"Morning, Zach."

"Usual thing?" Zach's smile is restrained but genuine. Always charming but can't hold on to it. Always looks away after eye contact lasts a second too long. "Branching out today?"

Hannah loves the flirty-shyness routine Zach does.

Just enough ego boost to get her through the morning. A little chitchat with the cute, shy barista before whatever hell the workday will bring raining down. Harmless fun. Deep down, she's sure Coffee God Zach does this bit with all the ladies who come in here. She'd like to think she's at least in the top ten of his favorites.

"No, no. No branching, please."

"Cool." Zach nods, moving toward the gleaming chrome grinder. "I'll bring it over."

"Thanks, man."

Hannah turns her attention back to what her sister is holding. A drawing of a pretty purple princess, perhaps? Maybe her little amazing Luna is going darker these days. A monster? Claws and fangs with some gore? That might be

refreshing, interesting, and delightfully disturb-
ing. She slides down into the chair across from
Corny. Loves that this place uses comfy,
unmatching chairs rather than the corporate
branding crap.

"Rough night?" Her sister scrunches her
nose.

"There's been rougher."

Corny smiles, looking her younger sister over.

She hasn't spoken to or seen Corny in weeks.
A lifetime for these two.

Hannah knows her evening is on full display.
All in her face. Her floating stare. She did her
best to fight back the red highways that stretch
across her eyeballs. Tried to hide the dark bags
under her eyes. But no question it's all there. Her
cheeks are probably a little puffy too.

While she did leave the happy hour before
mistakes were made, she also managed to polish
off a bottle of red in her apartment after she got
home. Dancing with herself and listening to
music until three a.m. Cheaper and better than
therapy.

"Still, you look great." Corny's face balls up
like she swallowed a bug. Hannah braces for the
blitz. "How can you party like a psycho rock-star
prom queen and still look like this? It took me

two hours to look like I jumped free from a car fire. You disgust me." Corny can't hold on to her fake disgust, breaks into a laugh.

"Oh, stop that crazy trash." Hannah waves off her sister's words. "You look fantastic."

"You're right, of course." Corny takes a sip. "I'm a freaking five-star MILF."

Hannah snorts a laugh. Her sister's deadpan delivery has always been a showstopper.

"What did lovely Luna make for me?"

"What?"

Hannah pushes her chin toward what's in Corny's hand. She can now see that it's a sealed envelope. A little formal for Luna. Upping her game.

"Oh this?" Corny gently places the envelope down in front of Hannah. "Not from Luna. Sorry. Although, now that you mention it, dear sweet Auntie Hannah, you should come out to the house this weekend. I realize traveling to north Austin crosses the border of cool, but Luna would love it. Maybe stay the night Saturday?"

"Maybe dry out?"

"That too. Couldn't hurt."

Hannah and Corny share a look. Non-verbal ammo fired off at a speed only sisters can do. Hannah knows everything her sister is thinking—

and implying—is out of pure, unfiltered love, but it still has lots of teeth.

They've had it out before about the way Hannah has been living with the pedal pressed down to the floor ever since the proverbial ink on the divorce dried. They've each said what they've had to say about the subject. No need to reheat it all.

Zach drops off Hannah's coffee on the table.

Thankful for the break in the war, Hannah touches his arm, then turns to Corny.

Zach closes his eyes off her touch.

"Corny, this is Zach. Zach, this is Corny."

"Nice..." He fumbles for something to say. Laughs off his awkwardness. "Good to meet you, Corny."

"It's Courtney. My sister is an asshole. But it's very nice to meet you too, Zach."

Hannah doesn't argue with the asshole assessment. Zach gives a quick nod then slips off, taking his place back behind the counter.

"That coffee dude might love you." Corny leans in with a grin. "Thought he might pass out when you touched him. You see his face?"

"Stop."

"You still seeing that healthy slab of male?"

"Gareth. Slab has a name."

"Fine. And?"

"Yeah, I guess I am. It's not serious, but I like him enough."

"Right." Corny starts to say something, stops, then starts again. "Are you still talking to that other guy?"

Hannah shrugs out a questioning posture.

"The therapist. I'm talking about the therapist."

"Oh, God no. Not anymore. He said I had control issues."

"He's right."

"That's what I said. Everybody knows that, so why do I need him?"

Corny opens her mouth, about to tear into her, but Hannah puts up a halting hand like a referee begging for calm.

"Let's not." Hannah flicks her wrist at her. "What's with the envelope?"

Corny's face wilts. She slumps back in her seat, looks down into her coffee.

"It's from Dad."

Hannah's shoulders inch up. She forces her teeth to stop from grinding.

"What?"

"What can I say? It is from Dad. I got one too. Saw him yesterday."

"Did you know you were meeting him?" Hannah can feel the temperature of her blood fire up. "Did you set it up or did he ambush you?"

"It was set up. Time and place."

"Oh? Didn't think to invite me?"

"Oh, I thought about it. Thought about how you might react the same way you are right now. Smoke is practically pouring out of you just talking about it."

"You been talking to him all along?"

"Come on. You really think that? This was the first time I've spoken to or seen him since he went bye-bye years ago."

"Mom know?"

"She got one too. She didn't want to discuss it."

"Shocking as hell."

"Yeah. She pretty much erased what I said to her as I was saying it. Oddly enough, she still took the envelope." Corny leans back in. "Look, I'll end the suspense. It's money. A check. I'm assuming you and I got the same amount, but I don't want to know if you got more."

Hannah slides the envelope back across the table to her sister.

"Stop." Corny pushes it back. "Take the money. That man left us with nothing." Grips her mug with both hands. "You remember Mom crying herself to sleep after her third shift at her second job? All those years scraping and clawing. School lunch programs. Rolling into school dressed in boys' hand-me-down clothes that didn't fit?"

"Cousin clothes." Hannah says it to herself as much as her sister. "They were such smug dickheads when they dropped them off too. Hated that—"

"Hannah." Corny shakes her head hard trying to knock loose a memory. "We can talk all day about that man and what he did but—"

"You remember him opening credit cards in our names after he left?" Hannah taps the envelope. "About ten grand each, if memory serves. Ruined our credit before we even had any."

"He started a new fund. Some big brain hedge fund. Maybe it was private equity... venture capital something... I don't know what it is. Point is, it's done well for him. He's not asking for a tearful reunion or your forgiveness."

"Right." Hannah holds her hands together to keep them from shaking. "Not yet."

"You don't even have to talk to him—I'll take that hit—but you need to take the damn money.

Pay off your student loans. Put a little away for that rainy day we hear so much about."

Hannah stares at the envelope. Her mind spins through her debts. Mountainous student loans. The twenty-two dollars and sixty-eight cents she has in her checking account. High interest-rate credit cards she used to buy a bed and a couch, not to mention the bar tabs and sushi she can't afford but pays for anyway to keep up with people from work. Prop up the appearance of belonging.

"How did he look?"

Corny's face forms a question mark.

"Is he aging well? Because Mom is still pretty hot, and if Dad is still looking okay, then I've got a long runway."

Corny knows where this is going, motions for her sister to bring it on.

"I mean you're half-dead. No offense, but locked down in the burbs married to a lawyer with a kid? You're as close to death while breathing as a woman can get. But this..." Hannah gently frames her own face between her hands. "This picture-perfect Hannah party can go on for years."

"Uh-huh." Corny's mouth forms a knowing smile. "You love little Luna."

"Guilty. Appreciate your sacrifice so I can have her in my life."

They clink coffee mugs.

"You're welcome. Look..." Corny's smile fades. She places her hands flat on the table, zeroing into Hannah's eyes. "I'd just like you to be kind of happy."

Hannah sips her coffee. A flashbang of thoughts.

All that she's put her sister through over the years. All the battles that still rage inside of her.

"Best I can do is sort of not sad."

THREE

HANNAH RUNS her fingers softly around the edges of the envelope.

Good quality.

Soft but still has a rough, rugged texture. Bone in color.

Dad always had a flair for the dramatic.

Like a check for an unknown amount delivered in a sealed envelope after years of neglect. Not as dramatic as walking out on his family after his hedge fund imploded during the great recession, leaving them with piles of debt while simultaneously draining the bank accounts without a word. Not even the courtesy of a bullshit *I'm sorry* note or a half-assed IOU. He literally said he was going to the store to get some milk. Hannah never saw him again.

She was thirteen. Corny was fifteen. Mom was devastated.

Hannah's stare hardens. She looks around the office, peeks above her cube walls to see if anyone is paying attention, or worse, coming her way. Only row after row of worker bees waiting out the clock. She breathes easy, drops back down into her chair.

She shakes the envelope, feeling the contents shift inside, hitting the corners. He obviously folded a piece of paper around the check to make sure the details were hidden from an easy look. Maybe the check is wrapped in the *sorry* note she's been waiting for. She punches her leg under her desk. Hard. Didn't even know she did it until her fist pulled away from her stinging thigh. Hates that she lets that man hold anything over her.

Even something as simple as an unapologetic *sorry*.

She saw a movie once—maybe it was in a book, maybe it was a book that was made into a so-so movie—where a guy was able to correctly determine the contents of an envelope just by asking a couple of questions. Not obvious ones like *What's in the envelope?* but more like things to narrow down the possibilities. She knows it's money, sure, but how much?

She starts at a number that makes sense. The ten grand he ran up on the card in her name when she was in junior high. He'd lied and said she was eighteen on the application. Said she worked at a burger place. Yeah, start at ten thousand and add the nineteen percent interest rate compounded over time. Then she adds the cost of college, then tacks on a trip to Disneyland she always wanted and a reasonable amount for braces she never got and clothes over the years. Then she doubles it and adds sixty-five percent just fucking because.

"Still not enough." She covers her mouth, spinning around in her chair to make sure her cubemates didn't hear her.

Hannah knows the only real question is how much is enough for her to forget where this envelope came from. To look past who signed the check. What's the number that will buy out the numbness? Renovate the void.

"You slipped away early."

Hannah almost breaks her eyes keeping them from rolling. The voice she abandoned last night at the bar is upon her. That know-it-all tone. The white-as-hell teeth. Neil, the okay computer genius guy from IT she'd left at the bar rather than shouldering the shame of an awkward morning. She soooo made the right choice.

"Sorry." She flicks her hair, giving him some big eyes. "I've got some projects this morning that I needed to be somewhat sharp for. You have a good time? Things get crazy after I left?"

"Not really. You were missed, though."

"Thanks."

Hannah lets the silence fill the office floor like a balloon. Neil clears his throat, then changes the subject to something about him. Several coworkers pass by, glancing their way. She knows the look. Rumor hounds wanting to see who's hooking up at work. *Keep moving, dogs of gossip.* Nothing to see here.

She looks to her phone, then back to the envelope. Feels a burning rise up from her stomach, flooding into her chest before reaching her face. The tips of her ears on fire. Neil is still talking but she can't hear a word he's saying. Nouns, verbs and adjectives bounce off her but there's that tone. A way he's looking at her.

Thinks of her ex-husband. Married too young. Divorced too late.

The way he'd talk to her, like she always needed to know something. Hannah watches Mr.

So-So Neil from IT. Studies his mouth moving. He pauses for a grin, as if he's an actor on a '90s sitcom waiting for laughs to end so he can deliver another line. Then he keeps going on and on. Nothing stacking on top of nothing.

She grabs her phone and stuffs the envelope inside her jacket pocket.

"So sorry, man," she says, halting Neil mid-sentence. "I gotta run. Forgot a super-special meeting."

Hannah rushes to the elevator without looking back.

As the doors close, her fingers work a text.

Working lunch?

Taps *send* to Gareth.

HANNAH PLANTS the palms of her hands down on his chest.

Nails dig. Head back. Grinds her hips on top of him until her skin sparks electric.

They'd said maybe four words to one another in the elevator up to her place. She went at him like her life depended on it. Gareth didn't fight it.

This is her working lunch. Her working it out. Her show to run. Her eyes slip back into her head as her lids close. Lips part, releasing a long, broken moan. Her body gives a final jerk before melting, sliding off his chiseled body. She'll take care of him later. Maybe.

Her hands fumble for the bottle of wine by the bed. She takes a gulp, then passes it over. Gareth declines the barely afternoon drinking. Hannah shrugs, takes another pull. He starts to say something. Hannah holds up a finger, requesting a moment.

"Feeling good is good enough for me. Talking can only damage this."

"Yes, ma'am."

They stare at each other, trying not to break their overly serious expressions.

Gareth rolls into a laugh.

So does Hannah.

"Dinner tonight?" he asks in that damn British accent. "I mean an actual meal. Not this. Not that this isn't wonderful."

She drifts for a moment. Steady stare into his crystal-blue eyes. Emotions flood, then freeze. A *yes* on the tip of her tongue, then quickly removed. Thinks of the envelope.

"No." She forces a regretful sigh in her voice. "Can't. Work thing tonight."

"Okay."

"Sucks. Sorry."

"No, no. I get it."

She can hear it dripping all over his words. He's not buying her ever-present, full-throttle crap. She also knows it's all she has to offer right now.

"Round two?" she asks.

Gareth nods.

OUTSIDE HANNAH'S BUILDING, the downtown streets are alive with midday hustle and bustle.

The white-collar elite with big-money attire tailored to appear as if they shop at a thrift shop. Service industry warriors who just woke up shuffle along in search of salvation tacos. All mixed in with the college kids from around the globe living the life youth and Austin have to offer them.

It's seventy and sunny today. Hannah hears it might be thirty and rainy tomorrow. Who knows? You could swim this afternoon and freeze to death tomorrow. Winter in Austin. As the old saying goes, *if you don't like the weather here... just wait.*

The sun shines down on Hannah, amplifying

her after-lunch glow. A cool breeze rolls across her face. She fixes her hair—messes Gareth's along with a peck on his cheek—then heads left down the street toward her office. Thinks maybe she'll grab another coffee on the way. Gareth goes right, pressing the button to unlock his slick, black monument to German engineering.

Zach watches from across the street, focused on the smirk on Gareth's face as he slides into that car.

His fingers tingle. Heart thumps. Feels the hum rattle into its maddening tickle.

Connect the dots, man. It's what's between the words.

It's the in-betweens that can save us. Or slaughter us.

FOUR

Hannah soaks in her oversized tub.

This is why she goes into debt for this apartment.

When she got home from work, she inhaled the leftover Thai she stole from a catered meeting upstairs—a meeting she wasn't a part of—then headed straight to her private sanctuary. This bathroom she keeps ER clean and this sweet, sweet tub. One of the two towels she owns waits on the closed toilet lid.

She can feel the water's warmth inside her bones. A shuffling playlist of The National plays from her bedroom as she sips pinot from a glass the size of her foot. As the wine rolls past her tongue and down her throat, she sets the glass down by the tub, leaving her fingers hanging down, touching the cool tile.

This is her time. Her escape from all of it. She'd purposely left her phone in the kitchen so any unsolicited buzzing wouldn't disrupt her oasis of wine, The National, and lilac-coated bubbles. She'd left the envelope in the kitchen as well. Still sealed. A still-unopened payoff from a man wanting to whittle down his sins.

To say it'd been a strange day is a severe understatement.

Hannah takes another drink.

She smirks, thinking how that unopened envelope is sitting next to a stack of unpaid bills. Ones she may never be able to remove from her ledger. Not completely. Shelling out monthly minimums, the accelerating various costs of life will keep her dishing out all of her so-so salary as quickly as it comes in. True, she can barely afford this apartment she's in, but living in this city costs real money and it's getting worse by the minute. Also, if she's being honest, this is really the only place she feels okay.

It's hers.

A place only a chosen few are allowed access to. A space she created for herself after years of not ever having anything. To call it furnished is a massive exaggeration, but she did buy a couch and the bed. The TV she got from Corny after they moved to the burbs. Sure, everything else in the apartment is a mix of deep discount stores and questionable people online, but they are things she picked. Things she chose to have.

As the melody of "Start a War" fades, she can hear her phone buzz. It's relentless. She imagines it bouncing on the kitchen counter like a hostile hornet's nest.

"Come on. Leave me alone."

Softly, she begs for the brief silence between songs to end so she can block out the buzz of her damn phone. It's probably Corny. She's already called three times and texted too many times to keep track of. Hannah knows the conversation before it starts, doesn't really feel the need to have it. Corny wants to talk about that man they technically call Dad. More importantly, she wants to talk about that envelope and tell Hannah what she already knows.

Corny will tell her to *stop with the bullshit pride. Understandable, but you need the money. Take the money and do not look back.*

Hannah isn't sure if she whispered all that to herself, acting it out in her best Corny voice, but that's exactly what her moderately older sister would say. What sucks the most is that she's probably right. Blowing some bubbles off her fingers, her thoughts shift to this morning.

To work. Neil. He'll make a fine pain in the ass for some other lucky woman. She thinks of her *lunch* with Gareth. What she needed. How she made that happen. How he asked to go to dinner. How she shrunk and then peeled away. Lied about a work thing tonight. After the divorce, after a ridiculous marriage, she made a solid, unbudgeable decision. A personal promise to herself to enjoy being young and free.

Never been the type to sleep around, despite the ugly cliché of daddy issues. Hannah has always thought in more of a monogamous sort of way. Not a moral or 1950s idea of what a nice, proper lady should be. For Hannah, it's always been more about peace of mind. One person to understand. One person to know and one to truly understand you. One to trust. All that, plus STDs scare the hell out of her. Aside from her ex-husband, who was her first in high school, she's only been with two other men. Gareth and a guy in her corporate orientation class when she was first hired.

She squeezes her eyes to close off the

memory of the orientation guy. Drinks some more wine.

"Crushing regret." Snickers to herself.

New job at a good company, and she had a bit too much to drink at a happy hour and slept with the cute guy who sat next to her in training. He of course told everyone, and that little mistake has led to a seemingly endless line of *Neils* at her cube. Can't blame anyone, really. She did what she did, but she'd like her workplace to move on from it like she has. That cute mistake from orientation doesn't even work at the company anymore. He texts from time to time when he's drunk. Hannah deletes them. Maybe she should leave her job and start somewhere else too.

Thinks of the envelope.

"Fuck that."

Snorts a laugh. Loves the absurdity of barking profanity out loud while alone, naked and covered in bubbles. "Fake Empire" fades out. The silent space between songs allows the buzzing of her phone to creep in again.

"Give it a rest, Corny. Good God, woman."

There's a knock at her door.

Loud, not timid or polite.

Jolts her in the tub, splashing water over the

edge. No one comes by her apartment, not even Corny. Certainly not at night.

Another booming knock rattles the walls. Whoever's out there had to work to get to her door. There's a keycard to use the elevator to reach her floor, and there's a doorman to get through to even get to the elevator.

Hannah sits up. "Who is it?"

"Hannah Rush?" The male voice is polite, but the tone is official. "My name is Detective Huston. I'm here with Detective Rebar. We're with Austin PD."

Hannah sits silent in the warm water. Head fuzzy from the wine. Heart cranking.

The knock at the door pounds harder.

"Miss Rush." A woman's hard voice cuts the air. Less polite. "Really need to talk to you. Something very bad has happened."

FIVE

"How do you know Zach Winter?"

Detectives Huston and Rebar sit in Hannah's living room.

She'd managed to throw on some joggers and a Longhorns sweatshirt. They showed their badges through the peephole. Hannah assumed they were real, but what the hell does she know about these things? Ever the polite hostess, she put on some coffee for her guests, the police detectives. Thought that offering them something might soften the mood of whatever this is.

Detective Huston is as big as a house. His thick hands show her a tablet, looking much like a gorilla holding up a paperback novel. He dresses like a slob but has a kind face. Huston taps and swipes until a picture of Zach lights up the screen.

Hannah's nerves pulse.

"You know him, right?" Rebar stands, leaning against the wall sipping her coffee looking like she wants to remove Hannah's heart with her fingers. "This Mr. Winter?"

Hannah tries not to be annoyed Detective Rebar didn't offer a thank you for the coffee. Huston did thank her, however, along with a thoughtful smile. A gentle giant sort of thing.

"Yeah, yes." Hannah stares into the screen. It's a so-so driver's license picture. "He works at a coffee shop I go to."

"You two seeing one another?" Rebar presses.

Hannah sees Detective Huston tense up. Not the way he'd go with this.

"*Seeing* one another?"

"You know what I mean." Rebar sips her coffee. "Dating. Romantically involved. Fucking?"

"Rebar." Huston holds up a hand. "Come on."

"No." Hannah swallows hard, not liking where this is going. "Like I said, he just works at a coffee place I go to. We talk every once and a while but I—"

"You go there a lot?" Huston tries to bring down the temperature. "This coffee place? It's down the street, right?"

Hannah nods. "Yeah. I go there pretty much every day before work."

"You flirt with Mr. Winter?" Rebar cuts back in. "Ya know, pretty much every day before work?"

"I'm sorry, have I done something wrong? I was taking a bath and you two—"

"Rebar, turn it down a little."

"You're not in trouble, Miss Rush." Rebar resets. Only slightly. "Just a conversation. Only trying to understand why a guy went into a house tonight, hacked up three people with a tactical blade, then got all cool and calm before he said he did it for you."

Hannah's mouth goes dry. Mind goes out of body.

"What... what are you talking about?"

Detective Huston leans back, closing the tablet. "Like she said—perhaps a little more direct than I'd like—Zach Winter entered a house tonight and murdered three people. We don't know why. But he did announce to God and anyone else listening that he did it for Hannah Rush."

She tries to speak. The words stick in her throat. What does a person say to that? She closes her eyes, runs her shaking hands through her still-damp hair.

"You need a minute, Miss Rush?" Huston's voice is warm and understanding.

"Yeah." Hannah sucks in a deep breath. She eyes her phone on the kitchen counter in the other room. "I think I might." Raising her cup, she gets up. "Can I get you some more coffee?"

Rebar stares back blank as can be. Huston nods a *yes* while mouthing a *please*.

Hannah takes Huston's cup and heads into the kitchen. Picking up her phone, she sees the screen lit up with texts and missed calls. Mostly from her sister, but there's another number mixed in too. No name. Not spam. She doesn't recognize it, but it is a 512 Austin area code. Hannah looks to her texts.

All she needed to see was the first few words of Corny's last text.

That coffee guy...

Hannah's mind spins. Knees turn to jelly. This isn't happening. How does her sister already know?

"Do you know a man named Gareth Hall?"

Rebar is now standing next to Hannah in the kitchen.

Jumping back, almost dropping her phone, Hannah's words now fight each other to get out. She manages a nod, wanting to ask *why*. Rebar cocks her head birdlike. For a fraction of a second, Hannah thought she saw a hint of humanity in the detective's eyes. It quickly fades, like a drop of rain landing in the desert.

Rebar's eyes bore through Hannah. "Gareth Hall was one of the three who were murdered tonight."

Hannah feels herself peel away from the here and now. Weightless, floating above herself, watching someone else being told these things. None of it making any sense.

"Where you romantically involved with Gareth, Hannah?"

A tear rolls down her trembling face.

What the hell is happening? The loose grip she held on her life is drifting away, like scraps of burning paper floating up and out into the night air.

She looks back to her phone. A single thought cuts through the chaos. A memory of a dinner conversation at her sister's months ago. Maybe a year ago. They were drinking wine and

Corny's lawyer husband said something. He was half-drunk but he offered the best advice he said a lawyer could give a person.

"We just want to ask you some questions, Hannah." Detective Huston now stands in the kitchen. They are on either side of her. "Really only want to get your point of view on all this."

Feels like they are closing in on her. Her chest tightens.

"Sounds like you've got a few guys in the wings, Hannah." Rebar smiles. "Sounds nice, if I'm being honest. Good for you. What happened? Zach find out about sexy Gareth and things went shithouse?"

"Am I under arrest?"

Rebar and Huston look to one another.

"No, Miss Rush, you are not." Huston smiles warmly again. "Like I said, just talking. Trying to understand what—"

"Great." Hannah taps her sister's number. "I'm calling my lawyer, and I'd prefer to not say anything more until he gets here."

"Pretty quick to lawyer up," Rebar sneers, looking toward her partner. "Screams out something to hide."

"Corny..." Hannah closes her eyes, bracing for the onslaught from her sister. "Courtney. I need you and Jake to come here now. The police are here." She nods. "Yeah, I know. I remember." Hannah locks eyes with Rebar. "I'm not saying a damn thing to them."

Hannah sets her phone down, fills Huston's cup with some fresh coffee, then hands it back to him. She did her best to keep her hands from shaking but her tough-kid routine only goes so far. Hannah hopes like hell she didn't tell these detectives too much already.

Huston waves off the coffee, all the warmth and kindness gone. There's a new coldness in his eyes that now matches Rebar's. They stand side by side staring back at her. Arms crossed. Daring her to make the next move. Hannah can't believe the good cop/bad cop cliché is a real thing.

"Feel free to stay, but like I said, I have nothing else to add. Not until my lawyer gets here."

"That how you want to go with this?" Huston asks.

Hannah stares back. "No comment."

Rebar shakes her head. "Really?"

"No comment."

Huston presses his lips together. Rebar is already heading for the door.

"I think that'll be it for now, Miss Rush,"

Huston says. "Of course, we will probably have some more questions for you. You may even have some questions for us. Maybe things you forgot to tell us."

Huston places his business card down on the counter, gives it a tap.

"Sorry for your loss." Rebar's voice is flat as she disappears out the door. "I mean losses."

Hannah wants to throw her coffee mug at the back of her head as she heads down the hall.

"Just so you and your attorney know." Huston moves toward the door. "As you might guess, this situation is all over the news and, more importantly, the internet."

Hannah's stomach drops.

Of course it is. Corny already knew. It's hit the news. Plastered all over every inch of the internet. Friends of her sister, people in her neighborhood probably all saw it while scrolling down social media. The doom scroll now includes Hannah Rush. People love sudden, freakish dramas that are someone else's problem.

"Hell." Huston shakes his phone. "Gotta a dumbass cousin in Tyler who shared the video about two minutes ago."

"Video? What are you talking about?"

"Some hipster clown caught it on his phone.

Probably lives on the same street or was walking through the neighborhood at the right time. It's not long, but the video shows Mr. Winter—covered in blood, of course—shouting out your name and everything."

Hannah's heart pounds.

"No comment."

"Lot of people love watching things on these little devil screens of ours. Sharing this stuff. Commenting on tragedy like it was a TV show. Kinda ridiculous way to spend your free time if you ask me." Huston lumbers to the door, then stops, checking the door and the locks. Turns the deadbolt, clicking it open and shut. The sliding, locking of the metal chills Hannah to the bone. "Whole lot of crazy out there."

"No comment." She can barely get the two words out.

"One other thing." Huston runs his finger over the door's security chain. "Zach Winter got away. We don't know where he is."

SIX

"THEY WERE JUST TRYING to shake your tree."

Hannah's brother-in-law stands in the center of the living room. No matter the time of day, Jake looks like a lawyer. Tall, clean cut, dark hair that's rarely out of place. A man born wearing a tie. Hannah always thought if Jake wasn't a real lawyer they'd pay him big money to be one on TV.

Corny hands Hannah a warm cup of tea.

"Well, it worked." Hannah takes the cup, thankful she has something to hold rather than keep covering her shaking hands. "Thank you for coming."

Jake waves off her thanks with an *of course, don't be silly* look.

"Drink the tea." Corny seemed to think

switching away from coffee was the better way to go considering her sister looked like she was about to jump out of her skin. No need to keep the volume turned up to thirty.

They got to the apartment about thirty minutes after Detectives Huston and Rebar left. Hannah can still feel their presence. Still hangs thick in the air. The sting of their stares. The weight of their words. The soul-leveling power of the news they delivered in their delightful detective sort of way.

"You did the right thing." Jake talks while thinking it all through. "Don't give them anything to work with. They aren't your friends with something like this. Even if you're completely innocent. They want to close the case as fast as possible and don't really care who gets steamrolled in the—"

"Okay." Corny flashes him a look. "We got it."

Jake puts up his hands, realizing he didn't read the room. Hannah appreciates his honesty. She's tougher than her sister thinks, but she'd like a moment to process without stark fear running rip-shit through her like a herd of hippos.

Jake is a good guy. Boring. But a decent, kind, stable person. Helped Hannah with her divorce when she had no money or anyone else to turn to. Corny would have killed him if he hadn't helped, but still. Corny always ran toward safety and comfort. Did her best to protect Hannah from everything—including protecting Hannah from Hannah—no matter how far Hannah might pull everyone down.

Corny had her share of wild days, of course, but at a certain point she just decided the party was over. Maybe it was when she met Jake. Maybe she was simply ready to meet someone like Jake. At this moment, Hannah's envy of boring and stable is punishing.

"I can't believe this is happening. He's just a guy at a coffee shop. He was nice." She turns to Corny. "You met him this morning. How? What—"

Corny puts her hand on Hannah's leg. Keeps quiet, letting her sister let it all go.

Hannah pushes it down instead.

Goes quiet. Too much to let run free. This is what she does. She knows it's not healthy, but she can't come undone. The one thing she learned after her father ran away—the only thing—is how to compartmentalize anxiety. Shove hurt into a basement of the mind and lock it all away no matter how hard it screams.

"Is it really everywhere?" Hannah sips her tea. "The video?"

Corny wraps her arm around her sister, squeezing tight.

"They think I drove him to it or something, don't they?"

"That's nuts." Corny squeezes tighter.

"Oh my God. They think I knew about it. That there was a plan or something or—"

"You did nothing wrong."

"But it's what they think, right? That's all that matters. They think I was sleeping with Zach and Gareth and there was this whacko love triangle, and I caused all this." Hannah gets up, starts wearing out a strip in the rug pacing back and forth. "That's the clickbait headline, right? That's the narrative that has everyone out there thumb-scrolling along."

Jake looks to Corny with a shrug. *She's not wrong.*

"Don't do this." Corny gets up. Tries to hug her sister again but stops as Hannah pulls away. "Don't read all that bullshit."

"But it's what's going around, isn't it?" Hannah balls up her fists. "Even if the cops don't leak it, the media will find out I was seeing

Gareth." She closes her eyes. "My job. They're going to fire me."

"They won't fire you." Corny turns to Jake. "They can't do that... can they?"

"It's complicated." Jake searches for the right way to say it. "They'll probably put you on paid leave at first just to avoid the circus. But if things escalate, who knows? Laws in Texas favor the employer so—"

"Not helpful," Corny fires back.

"You want me to lie to her? She's your sister, but she's my client now."

Hannah raises her arms, asking for peace.

The bedroom door cracks open. A perfect face peeks out, tiny hands rubbing her eyes. For a fraction of a second, everything that's happened falls away from Hannah's mind. Her heart melts just looking at her niece.

Perfect little Luna is here.

Corny and Jake brought her because they couldn't leave her alone at home. Luna and Corny had waited in the car until Jake found out the detectives were gone. Then they gave her an iPad, some headphones, and made her a comfy pillow world on the floor in Hannah's room. A so-so babysitter substitute but it was better than other alternatives.

Hannah didn't want to see her when Luna first came in. She couldn't. She was too raw. A swirling hurricane of emotions and fear. Hannah hid in the bathroom until she knew little Luna wouldn't see her like that.

The images a child sees can burn into memories for life. Hannah still remembers the look on her father's face when he left. She'll never forgot it. The coldness in his eyes as he acted like nothing was going on. *Just running to the store.* There's no way she wants Luna's memories of her to be at her worst moment. A horrific framed picture of Hannah unhinged in her niece's mind.

With her arms wide, Hannah begs Luna for a hug.

Never needed something so bad in her life. Luna's little feet thump the floor and she launches face-first into her aunt's open arms. A part of the world still makes sense. Hannah exhales for what seems like the first time in forever.

"Guh. You're crushing my bones," Luna says.

"Sorry." Hannah releases. "Too much?"

"Never too much." Big smile. "Are you in trouble, Aunt Han?"

Hannah smiles huge, both at the question and

Luna's name for her. She couldn't say it correctly when she was really little, so she just went with Han. Being a massive *Star Wars* fan, Hannah couldn't have been happier with Luna's translation.

"Not trouble—" Corny steps in.

"I am," Hannah cuts her off. She decided a long time ago she would never, ever lie to Luna.

"Big trouble?" Her little voice cracks.

"Not sure yet. Nothing I can't handle, though."

"Because you're tough." Luna's eyes go big, putting an exclamation point on *tough*.

"Try to be, but I do need some help."

"Can I help?"

Hannah nods. "I need you to be you and give hugs whenever they are requested. A zero-sass policy. Can't ever say no, either."

"Hmmm." Scrunches her nose. "Think I can do that."

"Good."

They shake on it. Luna wraps her thin arms around Hannah's neck, then bounces back to the bedroom, waving as she shuts the door. Hannah's shoulders inch back up to her ears. She feels every muscle in her body pull tight. Her mind spins back to the chaos. The questions. The fumbling, falling feeling, unable to find stable ground beneath her.

"You should get her home to her own bed."

"I'm not going to leave you here like this," Corny says.

"I'm fine. There's nothing we can do right now anyway."

Corny looks to Jake, who shrugs. *She's not wrong.*

"Look. Call us in the morning," Jake says. "Don't go in to work. I'll walk you through what to say to them."

Hannah nods, numbness starting to set in.

"Actually, don't talk to anyone. Certainly not reporters. Matter fact, don't leave this building." Jake thinks. Lowers his voice in case Luna is listening. "That guy is still out there, but don't worry. He'll make mistakes, the cops will find him. But I'm asking my firm to put some people outside your building. Just to be safe."

Hannah gives a thumbs-up. Whispers a thank you.

Corny holds Hannah's hand. "The world has a remarkably short attention span. Maybe if we stay quiet, ride this out, it'll all fade into the background. Something else will get the clicks. The cops will find out that you had nothing to do with any of this and it will all melt away."

"Maybe a new war can start or something." Hannah's smile is forced and broken. "Alien invasion?"

"We can hope."

"Am I still invited to the house this weekend?" Hannah looks to the closed door that Luna went into.

"Of course."

Hannah fights back turning into a puddle on the floor. Bites her lip. Simply knowing that somewhere safe still wants her, it's almost too much in the moment.

"One thing." Corny raises her sister's chin gently with her finger and thumb.

"Yeah?"

"Don't bring a date."

Hannah chokes on her laugh.

PART TWO

SEVEN

Zach stares into the mirror.

Clumps of his hair lay in the sink. A roach scurries up the wall.

He taps the electric clippers against the side of the counter, knocking loose some hair stuck in the number two guard he'd attached. They said he should cut his hair "tight." Some said even bald. Anything to dramatically change his look. Some asshole said something about only wearing hoodies.

Amateurs go with hoodies. That silenced the group.

Connect the dots, man.

It's what's between the words. It's the in-betweens that can save us. Or slaughter us.

He made the call to cut his hair just off the

skull. Clean, radically different from his shaggy coffee-guy look. Shaved his face too. They said to get some glasses if you can't get your hands on colored contacts. Both together works even better. Get some fake tats for your neck. That will get you past the vast majority of eyeballs for at least the next day or so. Takes the cops and feds time to update and adapt. They need to understand what they're dealing with. They will hunt hard and fast the first couple of days because they will assume they are dealing with something less than what you are.

Make no mistake, they will underestimate you like they always do, Zach.

That's how you win.

Zach applies a thin sheet of paper to his neck while reading the instructions on the temporary tat. He'd gone with a simple black design that looks like thorns. Something you'd see around town in the service industry or inked on someone in a band. Austin is swimming with them.

In the room next door, through the thin walls he can hear a man and woman having sex. Been going at it for a while. They've been drinking, too. Can hear the bottles and laughs between the thumps and moans.

Zach hopes they're having fun.

He picks up a pair of black glasses. The type he's seen tech guys wear when they come into the coffee shop. As he tries them on, he smiles big in the mirror, then drops his grin immediately. He got what he wanted. Look unlocked. He looks like a common coder dope but that was the idea.

His mom told him once, *You ain't special. Who you fooling? You're just wrong.*

Sister said the same, only worded slightly better. His brother went ghost years ago. Ever since the accident—or *accidents*—depending on who you talked to they weren't accidents at all—after those, things changed in a big way. Subtle changes at first, but subtle began to swell into big, then bigger than big. He did what he did to that kid in the lunchroom that one time sophomore year. No one ever looked at him the same way.

Zach said he was sorry. Said he was wrong. Promised to be better.

But when something happened later—it was a different *accident* but they all said it was exactly the same—then they talked about getting him on pills on top of pills. Said there were doctors he could talk to. So much talking about nothing.

He tried it for a bit. Some of the pills made him feel like a deep, empty pit. Made his mind fuzzy at times. As if his soul was removed and replaced by an older model that didn't work as well.

All of it numbed his buzz. Dulled his hum.

Now, Zach just stays quiet. Doesn't speak to any of them. Family or friends from before are barely memories now. As if he tapped mute on the voices he doesn't want to hear anymore. Keeps his thoughts mostly to himself. Shares a bit of himself anonymously online.

Behind him, one of the local stations plays reruns of whatever on TV.

The bed in the room next door is rhythmically thumping the wall. The guy grunts. The woman requests more. The image of Hannah and Gareth flashes. He can see them in the mirror. As if they magically appeared on a big glass screen that takes up the bathroom wall. The two of them together this afternoon walking out of her building. She looked so distant and lost. He seemed so smug. So impressed with himself.

Zach studied the layout of that house online. He thought about starting with a warning, but he knew that guy—that Gareth—wouldn't listen. Too much ego. Knew he'd be wasting his words, but Zach still thought he needed to try. After all, he isn't some psycho on a killing spree. He can still hear them laughing. The way they sounded before he walked into the house. Sounded like children mocking. Relentless cruelty in their laughs.

Memories of moments swipe and tear at his mind.

He'd slipped in through an unlocked door at the back of the house that led into the kitchen. The hum cranked up to another level. He just kept slicing and stabbing until he got to a man. That guy. Gareth, the architect of Hannah's sadness.

No showdown moment. No final words spoken.

Zach doesn't even remember killing him. Only recalls seeing the body slump down to the floor. Eyes wide. Amazed. Confused.

All he'd wanted was for someone to listen to him. To see him.

He reviews all the training he did in his tiny apartment. Once he'd entered the living room, all mental reps of his knife work took over. Muscle memory kicked in. He'd spent so much time practicing his grip. His strikes. Time spent at the gun range. Bullets punching holes in paper heads and hearts.

In the mirror, he watches it all play out in

front of him, the mirror's surface showing his mind projecting a show only he can see. The house. Their faces contorted in fear. All the sensations come rushing back to him. His mind keeps bouncing back. Rewinding. Replaying it all no matter what he does.

He sucks in a deep breath, calming himself. He did what he had to do. Tonight, Zach finally took the step.

A big one.

He knows they were right all along. His real friends. Faceless and without true voices, but they are the only ones out there in the world to support him. To guide him, tell him how to act. Steps to take. Actions needed.

Zach's fingers tingle. His heart thumps. Feels the hum begin rattling its maddening tickle.

The shower he took felt nice, although it was hard to relax when he thought the cops would kick in the door at any second. Even then, as the warm water had poured over him, he couldn't stop replaying it all. The look in their eyes. The blood that poured. The screams.

His palms slam down on the counter.

The wall shakes. He tosses the glasses to the counter, squeezing his eyes closed and thrashing his head hard side to side. Bumps rise up along his bare skin. His eyes open. The mirror is back to showing only him. Just over his shoulder, he can see the TV behind him.

The local news stopped talking about him. At least for now. In a few days, maybe less, they won't say anything at all. His plan will take some time. He knows he needs to be flexible. Adapt or die. This is a fluid situation. He checks his watch. The tat needs a little more time before it's ready.

He'd thought what he did at Gareth's house would be harder than it was.

Thought he'd feel bad. He doesn't know what he thinks about it. Not really. There was a pang of shock as it was happening, but then there was this lift away from himself. A separate, alternate self emerged, watching what Zach was doing. No judgement, only a piece of Zach left there for support. A friend to guide him through the difficult work. Help him past the frightened looks of everyone in the house. The disbelief that this was happening to their perfect lives.

Then it was over.

Zach had dumped the internet-perfect woman's Audi at a park a few miles from here. Handpicked this cheap motel north of Austin, didn't want to drive too far. Not smart to be on the road out in the open with a hostage in a stolen car. He knew it wouldn't take long for them to piece together her name and her car. She'd screamed and begged. Cried hard for her life to remain intact.

What life? Zach thought. An endless quest to blow guys for money without the courage to call it what it really was.

He'd thought about killing her when he left the car. Leaving a live witness seemed like an amateur move, but he realized she didn't know anything about him. He hadn't said a single word to her. As disgusting as she was, she didn't deserve to be killed. Maybe she'd take this as a wakeup call. He's getting a real taste for this, but he's not a psycho. So, he left her in the car with her eyes covered and her hands zip-tied in the back seat, then ran hard in the darkness to this dump of a motel. Paid cash and went to work on his appearance.

He checks his watch. Almost tat time.

His mind shifts to Hannah.

Imagines her alone, looking at her phone, scrolling through the news of what he's done. Staring into the screen of the phone he's seen her look into so many mornings at the coffee place. Only this time, she's looking at him. Seeing him and who he is. Not some servant fetching an acceptable drug for the masses.

She'll see him again real soon.

As he turns toward the TV, he sees Hannah's building behind a reporter. He needs to hurry. There are already eyes on her. The vultures are circling.

He's seen the posts on the site he goes to every day. Thoughts and comments streaming down like rain. They all said they were friends, but he knows some of them can't be trusted. Lots of great information. Tips and tricks for what Zach is doing. Like having multiple laptops with VPNs. He'll need to nuke the hard drive on the one that's sitting on the bed. He needs to be connected but don't use one too long. The first few hours and next few days are hyper-critical to success or failure.

Connect the dots, man.

It's what's between the words. It's the in-betweens that can save us. Or slaughter us.

Checks his watch, peels off the paper, revealing his new tat. Slips the glasses back on. He needs to leave this room just before the sun starts to come up. He'll go into the room next door while the two lovebirds are sleeping it off and take their truck. It's a blue Ford that looks like every other blue truck around here. Perfect. He has a stash of supplies hidden a few miles from here.

If the lovebirds see him—and most likely they will—he'll be forced to kill them.

Doesn't want to.

He's not a psycho.

But he'll do what he has to do.

EIGHT

IT's three in the morning.

Hannah has been pacing the meager square footage of her apartment ever since Corny and Jake left. It's been hours, she's not sure how many, and while she knew peace of mind wasn't really an option, she was not prepared for the quiet that filled her space.

The silence is deafening.

One minute she wants to escape. Run screaming out into the street. The next she wants to curl up into a ball in the corner and wish it all away.

She's done all she could to avoid the news. Her phone. Made the mistake of checking her email.

Mixed in with the spam and relentless

retailers claiming once-in-a-lifetime savings were emails from the few friends she has. All of them forwarding links to local news feeds. Some had screen grabs from social media. One had a fuzzy, close-up picture of Zach in front of Gareth's house. Arms up. Red and blue lights glowing all around his face.

Hannah considered uncorking a new bottle of wine. Open it up, dump it down her throat until she feels nothing. Let the bottle drain to slow the world from tearing her apart. Until there was some semblance of control. Then Hannah could have a say in her state of being. Not a great choice, but it would at least be her poor decision to get hammered.

After a deep stare into the bottles, she pushed away from the collection of poor decisions calling for her in her kitchen. She's spent the last few hours spinning through some mindless rom-coms and some even more mindless reality TV staples.

Focus has become joke.

Even the simplest of entertainment concepts have failed her. Images and sounds smear into a mess of clicks and clacks that rattle in the background while her switchblade mind cuts through everything that's happened. So she turned off the

TV but couldn't find the off button for her thoughts.

The things the detectives said. The look on their faces. The tone they used.

That cold, cutting statement that Zach is still out there. Roaming. Unchecked.

Was there something she could have done to stop this? Did she cause this, even in some small way?

She knew sleep wasn't a possibility, for more reasons than she can count, but the most glaring reason almost put her on the floor.

The last time she was in her bed was with Gareth. The bedroom still felt like him. The feeling of sex and playful sin is still there. She shakes her head hard. Needs do something to break her mind loose from the spiral. She picks up her phone, ignores the burning red numbers letting her know all the texts and messages she's missed. She taps a name.

"Corny." Hannah's voice crackles. "I'm going to do some laundry."

"What?" Groggy but trying to sound awake. "What the hell are you—"

"It's like ten, maybe fifteen steps down the hall." Hannah wrestles her laundry basket while balancing the oversized detergent bottle, pausing to pick up stray socks and such that fall, creating a jagged trail behind her. "And you're going to stay on the phone with me while I do it."

"Okay. Okay." Corny is moving. Hannah thinks she's probably heading downstairs to avoid waking up the rest of the house. "Take something with you."

"Like what?"

"I don't know. Like something to defend yourself with. Inflict pain on others."

The idea sends a chill through Hannah. Makes perfect sense. Of course it does. Solid advice from her sister. What bothers Hannah is the fact that she needs a weapon to do laundry. Looking around her place, she stops, then leans the basket up against the refrigerator. Buys herself a half second so she can pull the biggest butcher knife she owns from the block on the counter and drop it on top of her sheets.

"Done."

Hannah didn't pay to have a washer and dryer in her apartment, which makes her unit one of the cheapest in the building. Cheapest real estate in a good neighborhood was the thinking, even though she can't even really afford this so-called cheap scrap of square footage. She still struggles with the idea that where a person washes their clothes is a measure of status.

"You still there?" Hannah stumble-rushes with her basket down the hall. "Corny?"

"Yes. Did you lock your door?"

"Yes." Rolls her eyes, sets down her basket, then moves quick to lock her front door. "Of course I did."

Hannah takes big, almost jumping steps down the hall. She peeks in. Thankfully, at this time of night the stark white, ultra-modern laundry room is empty, rows of washers and dryers waiting with mouths open wide. She sets the knife next to the basket, then shoves the sheets and pillowcases into one washer. Tears fall in drop by drop. She didn't even know she was crying.

"You okay?" Corny asks.

"Absolutely not." Hannah wipes a fat tear away. "But I'm not being attacked if that's what you mean."

"Considering the night you've had, we'll call that a win." Corny sips what Hannah guesses is a new pot of coffee. "Now, start that damn laundry and get back to your place."

Hannah stuffs her bed-in-bag comforter into another washer, then dumps a cup of thick, blue detergent into each before jam-feeding quarters into the slots. She'd grabbed a handful from her life-savings jar on the way out the door. Can't help but smile at the fact she snatched up just enough quarters without counting. Corny's right—gotta take the wins as they come.

"Thank you, Corny."

"For what?"

Hannah knows her emotions are dancing at the tips of her fingers. She would never say this under normal circumstances, but she doesn't care.

"For everything. Not sure I've ever said that."

"You have not, but it was never a requirement. You get the lifelong gift card for my help."

Hannah's tears roll again, only now they slip and fall over her half a smile.

"Feel like I've maxed out that card sometimes."

"Nonsense."

As the machines start up, the soft whirling provides Hannah with the perfect white noise she didn't know she needed. Taking a deep breath, she soaks up the stillness of the room. The calm. The eye of the storm.

"I think I'm okay." She touches the butcher

knife, then places it into the basket. "I'll call you in the morning."

"I'll stay on."

"No, I'm good. Get some sleep."

"I'm up anyway so—"

"It's fine. I promise. I've got a knife and a phone. Plus, I'm remembering a lot from that class we took a few years ago."

"The *go for the balls and eyes first* class."

"Then the knees."

"Ahh yes, the knees."

"I'm good." Hannah swallows hard. Finds a brave voice. "Don't worry."

"*Don't worry*, she says. Yeah right. No problem." She hears the sound of Corny's TV. "Call me when you get back to your apartment. In like three minutes or less. Don't sit there waiting on your clothes."

"Okay."

"Not kidding. Two minutes or less."

"Okay. I will." Hannah smiles at the fact Corny subtracted a minute as she taps an end to the call.

Staring at the machines as they hum, her shoulders start to come down inch by inch. The small green light at the top of the washer blurs as she lets her eyes go in and out of focus trying to jar loose the events of the day. The simple act of doing laundry has been therapeutic for her over the years. Taking care of the clothes she owns. Respecting what they cost and what it takes to pay for them. This was always a quiet moment for her during her week.

Tonight is different. No way to avoid it.

Tonight? This is the act of trying to wash away what she can't comprehend. She could still smell hints of his aftershave on the pillow. Then it hits her like a tsunami.

What if she'd said yes to dinner?

Hannah braces herself, planting hands on the washer.

Her knees simply give out from under her. She fights to bring air back into her lungs. She could have prevented this. All she had to do was just have dinner with the good-looking guy she liked. He'd asked her a question that a million women would have said yes to. If her damaged brain had allowed her to enjoy her life, maybe he'd be alive. If she had simply allowed something possibly good into her life—*what the hell is wrong with her?*

Blotches form at the corners of her vision. The world tilts.

Corny's voice starts up inside her head. No

need to have her on the phone. She can hear her say, *Not your fault, Hannah.*

"It is," she says, barely above a whisper. "I did this."

Zach did what he did on his own... and if it wasn't tonight, he would have done this horrible thing some other time.

"I flirted with Zach every morning. I did too much."

Bullshit. Being nice to a guy at a coffee shop doesn't make you responsible for him killing people. You know that. Stop this. You did nothing wrong.

"Okay." Hannah bites her lip. Spreads her hands flat on the washer. Fingers stretched wide feeling the cool metal. She lowers her head down, resting it on top of her hands. Lets her sister's imagined words flow. "Okay."

She thinks of the few therapy sessions she did go to.

Would never admit it to Corny, but there was some good in there. Some of it was helpful. There was lots of talk about focusing on what Hannah has control of. The guy went on and on, it was brutal at times, but he attacked the issue from different angles. An issue Hannah would rather avoid like hell. The theme was always the same—the illusion of control. How she can't control what others do, only herself. Perhaps the hardest person on the planet to get her arms around.

She breathes in deep, filling up her back, counting to three, then exhaling, pushing out the crazy. Something he showed her. Doesn't take much. Taking just a moment to slow the rambling mind. Something to try when the anxiety spikes. When life gets slippery. When control feels lost, take a breathing, resetting pause. Sometimes it even works. But...

"Not today," slips out from her lips.

"Pardon?"

Hannah spins off the washer, almost putting her on the tile floor. Her back bounces off the wall. Eyes wide and wild, she puts her hand on the knife.

"Hey, no. Sorry."

A man stands in the laundry room doorway. Looks to be fighting the wrong side of forty with a stylized mop for hair. Hannah's spiking fear comes down. Only a little. He's not exactly an imposing figure, and she has a big-ass knife, but Hannah's heart still beats against her ribs like a drum.

She does know there's more than a few

recently divorced, middle-aged dads living in the building. All hoping for one last shot at life by overpaying to live in a *cool building* in downtown A-Town.

He holds his body in the universal pose that he means her no harm. Open hands where she can see them. Keeps his distance. The man adjusts his denim jacket, pulls at the collar of his T-shirt, adjusts his wire-rimmed glasses, then finds some charm.

Big smile with raised eyebrows asking *are we cool?*

Hannah moves off the wall as her breathing levels off to some semblance of normal. Keeps her hand on the knife.

"Wow. You scared the hell out of me." He extends a hand. "Alex Nord. I was just kinda up and about. Heard you in here. Thought someone was, you know, causing problems in the building."

Hannah stares at his hand as if it were made of fire but manages a tight wave.

"Just washing my stuff, man."

"Can see that." Alex leans a little closer. "You look familiar."

"Yeah. I live in the building."

"Right. Sure. No, it's something else."

"Okay. I really just want to do this—"

"Not sure what it is, but you look like someone... Oh well." Alex shrugs, then thumbs toward the window. "You see all the crazy shit going on outside?"

"Look, man." Hannah feels her chest tighten. "I just want to wrap up some laundry here and then get some sleep. It was super nice talking to you, Alex."

"Sure. Sure. Good to meet you..." Leaves it hanging, waiting for her to say her name.

"Goodnight, Alex Nord. Pleasure."

"Got it." Nodding, he slips out the door without another word.

Hannah counts to ten. Tries some more breathing. Doesn't work.

Now she's amped up even more than before. More creeped out than ever. He recognized her.

Does he know her from the building? Did he recognize her off something he saw on his phone and then went looking for her?

All the frightening possibilities roll through her mind. He said something about all the crazy outside the building. She hadn't even opened the curtains in her apartment, let alone looked out the window. Her eyes move toward the window on the other side of the laundry room.

With careful steps, knife gripped in her fist, wanting to see but not wanting to see, she peeks out through the blinds. Down below outside the building are vans and SUVs with various local television station logos on the sides. Men and women scurry around holding microphones and cameras. A small crowd of onlookers have their phones raised, capturing every angle of the night.

She's only a few stories up but they look like bugs. Moving, swarming, and worst of all...waiting. One of the cameramen tilts his camera up. A woman in a cocktail dress holding her shoes by the straps points her phone up toward the building. Right where Hannah is standing.

Hannah drops down to the tile.

She curls up into a ball in the corner, trying to stay out of sight. She'd like nothing more than to fall into a hole and disappear. Maybe go back in time and make this all go away. The walls are pushing in on her as she fights to find air to breath.

You have to get back to your apartment.

Crawling on her hands and knees on the cold tile, she makes her way toward the door. This was a stupid idea. She should have stripped down the bed and tried to sleep on the bare mattress, or maybe used that too-small lap blanket she uses in the living room in front of the TV. She could have made a pillow world on the floor like Luna.

Luna.

A flash of an image of her perfect face jolts Hannah back into the here and now.

She needs to pull it together. Didn't ask for any of this but it's on her. If she can just get back to her apartment, she can lock the door and close out the world. Maybe long enough to try and make some sort of sense out of this. Maybe she can just wait it out, like Jake was talking about. He's probably right, but she now knows she can't wait and wish this all away.

This might be the kind of story that has some staying power. The media, the people, the wandering minds of the bored do love to dig into some stories for years and years.

Is mine one of those stories?

She needs to know what's being said out there. Needs to face the information that's being streamed and digested by the masses. Can't change any of it, but she needs to know what's out there so she can form a plan. Maybe prepare for the fight that's coming. Whatever that may mean.

She stops her crawl. Sucks in a deep breath.

On the floor where Alex Nord stood is a card. A stark white business card.

With shaking hands, Hannah picks it up. There's a handwritten note with a phone number on the back.

There's a lot you need to know, Hannah.

NINE

Hannah shuts her apartment door behind her.

Locks every lock.

Stops. Checks them again before setting her new favorite butcher knife on the kitchen counter.

The blinds are half closed but open enough for a quick peek. She only hopes it's enough to keep the vultures from getting a good look at her. No doubt they've figured out which apartment is hers. Right about now, she's wishing she'd paid up for the washer and dryer and hadn't *lucked out* with a view of the city.

Taking a single deep breath in, as if diving deep underwater, she stabs her finger harder and harder at her phone's glass, moving farther and farther down the infinite scroll. Eyes glaze past all the links, the seemingly endless list of stories and posts about what's happened tonight. A wildfire spreading across the internet. Searing its place into the minds of the bored and disenchanted across the city. Across the country. Hell, the entire damn planet.

Zach Winter's picture from his driver's license is everywhere. There's also a picture of him off the coffee shop's website. His crooked smile hits her. The eyes she'd thought were kind. She stops her scroll as her stomach falls through the floor.

"Shit."

Hannah's reached a place she knew was inevitable. Another picture that's been peeled off social media. Several. All of her.

There's one where she's smiling nice and sweet—*the set-up pic.*

Another shot of her drinking at a party and talking to some guy—*building their story.*

Then another with her laughing, arm around the guy from her training class, a massive glass of wine in hand—*the kill shot.* She scans the words. It's like the digital collective is building a character sketch of Hannah Rush without knowing anything about her.

She slides down the wall, taking a seat on the

floor. The reality of it all rains down. As if every set of eyes in the world are staring at her right now. At a version of her she never agreed to. Never offered up. But one that is just true enough to be plausible. They've pulled together pieces from different times in her life to back up whatever they want her story to be.

All the taps and clicks around the world cut and carve away at her. She wants to put her phone through the wall. Scream until her throat bleeds. Her entire life has come undone in a matter of hours. Her phone has been buzzing so much she had to silence it completely. Hard to hold and read with so many texts and calls roaring in. Most are numbers and names she doesn't recognize.

There's that 512 number that she's seen a few times. No name. Still can't place it. Has to be a damn robo spam annoying asshole call.

Then CORNY pops up big and bright.

Shit. Hannah forgot to call when she got back to her place. Another deep breath before she answers.

"Here's the video everyone is talking about."

Hannah stops short of accepting her sister's call, turning toward the TV that she forgot she'd left on. From the floor, she moves toward the velvet voice and helmet of hair that's talking on the local news.

Her eyes squeeze closed.

She's been avoiding watching what Detective Huston told her about. She's speed-scrolled past the video online the best she could. The last thing she's shielded herself against. Worked so far, but she knows the unavoidable is upon her.

She must see it.

Holds her breath.

Opens her eyes.

The video tilts, then straightens slightly before bobbing up and down. Zach stands in the yard of a sprawling home. One she guesses is Gareth's. There are sirens screaming in the background, but you can see and hear the police trying to talk to Zach.

Her hand creeps up, covering her mouth.

Corny calls again. Hannah taps it away.

The video pushes in. Zach's eyes are wild and wide, blood sprayed across his face as bright red and blue police lights strobe. He's holding a gun to the head of an attractive, terrified woman. Her eyes are closed, black mascara-tears streaming down her face. Two people move into frame. Detectives Huston and Rebar. They were there for it all.

"Hannah," Zach calls out.

The tiny hairs at the back of her neck stand tall.

"Hannah Rush." Louder. Harder.

Her body trembles. Still hanging on to the hopeless hope this isn't happening.

"Hannah!" He screams like a caged animal, spit flying. Then, as if a string was pulled, he slams into a chilling calm. "I did this for you."

Hannah stands motionless, staring at the screen but seeing nothing. Hollowed out. Gutted. Something reached in and ripped away everything she is, leaving her with only a husk of what she was before tonight. What she will ever be.

Through the lights from the police cars, the headlights, and everything else, Hannah catches a quick glimpse inside the house. The woman on the news draws viewers' attention to it, even goes as far as asking her people to slow it down and blow up the image.

"There. Right there you get a peek into the horror that took place inside that house."

Hannah's knees give.

"Chilling to see—"

The cotton-candy voice of the news anchor dissolves to the back of Hannah's mind.

She wilts down, grabbing the end of the

couch before hitting the floor. In the shadows of the house, she can see the bodies. Hannah's head drops, looking away from the screen. Self-defenses saving her from herself. Her fingers fumble finding the remote, punching off the TV.

The room goes quiet.

Silent save for the faint hum of the chaos outside in the street. Her grip on the here and now is failing her. Nothing connecting. Emotions burn white hot, then disappear as fast as they ignited.

She rolls onto her back, staring up at the ceiling. Memories spin and whirl at blinding speed. Some play in some form of order. Others don't. All the times she walked into the coffee place. The mornings she talked to Zach. She smiled. He smiled back. Jokes casually tossed about. Then her mind twists to thoughts of her father. Her and her sister growing up with a mom who was broken. Last, the searing image of the bodies on the floor inside the house behind Zach. The horrible calm on his blood-sprayed face.

"Stop," commanding the ride to end.

She wants off.

Pushing herself up off the floor, Hannah stumbles into the kitchen. Opening the freezer, she finds the bottle of Tito's she keeps there. She pours a shot of chilled vodka into a jelly jar glass, then throws it back.

Really? Corny's voice rattles in head. *So not the time for this shit.*

"Not sure there's a better time."

Hannah lets the booze work the magical chill-burn as it slips its way down. Thoughts slide away from the video, from everything that's happened, before landing on a conversation with her therapist. The last visit she had with him before she walked away from *working on herself.*

He kept at her no matter how many wiseass barriers she threw in front of him. Beating the same drum, for the ten thousandth time, he talked about her anxiety. The arresting fear that she can't control her tiny hills of happiness and deep valleys of sadness. She'd cut him off—putting up a stop-sign hand, halting him midsentence from his well-meaning words—and asked him the one question she'd always wanted to ask someone. She'd crafted it years ago, waiting for the prefect person to hurl it at.

"What are we expected to do with all this dismal fate?"

He looked at her. Eyes sinking. Coughed, cleared his throat. Hiding his exhaustion while listening.

"*All of us, every single day, pretending we're not born to die. Kind of dumb, don't you think?*"

"*Hannah, this is what we've been talking about. You're right to a certain degree, but—*"

"*I know. I get it. Power of positive thinking and all that. But this isn't about the hopelessness of life. What I'm struggling with is that there has to be something I can do in the meantime, ya know? Have some fun in the precious moments between now and the horrible shit to come.*"

Hannah pours another punch of Tito's.

She remembers walking out of the office, leaving the therapist with little to say. She never went back. He was a good guy. Smart. Kind. A good therapist who genuinely wanted to help her, but Hannah wasn't there. Tried it on for size because Corny asked her to, but it just didn't fit.

She'd had no idea how right and wrong she was that day.

The precious moments between now and the horrible shit to come had been so much shorter than she anticipated. And the horrible is much more horrible than she could have imagined. Had her fun brought it all on?

You did nothing wrong. This is not on you. Corny's voice pleads with her to listen.

"Yeah, yeah." Another pull of Tito's.

There's a hard knock at her door.

Hannah drops the jelly jar glass to the counter, catches it before it shatters to the floor, whips her head around to the sound. It was a single knock, then another. Hannah makes herself like a hole in the universe. No idea what time it is. It's late, or early. Has to be creeping up on four or five in the morning. Holding her breath carefully so as not to make a sound, she inches toward the peephole.

Looking out, she sees nothing. A tunneled vision of an empty hallway. Toys with the idea of opening the door and taking a look. Balls her fists tight.

She exhales. "The hell with that."

Doublechecking the locks, she moves back to the kitchen, mind bouncing once again.

Was it a reporter? That weird guy from the laundry room?

Zach?

They said they can't find him. Hannah picks up her knife. Feels better just having it in her hand. The envelope from her dad sits unopened on the counter next to the vodka bottle.

The edges around her sight are starting to blur ever so slightly. Her head floats, stomach turns. The events of the day and the Tito's are

doing a number on her. She touches the envelope, still impressed by the quality dear old Dad
purchased. She picks it up, wondering the dollar
amount in there.

Is it enough to disappear on?

Did he give her the best gift at the best time
without even knowing it? Can she somehow take
this money and go ghost, leaving all this
behind her?

She has to get out that door first.

Past whatever, whoever might be out there
waiting for her.

Corny calls again. Hannah knows she has to
answer.

"What the hell? Are you okay?" Corny's
words are hardened by worry.

"I'm okay." She clears her throat. "I'm back to
my place."

"Don't sound okay."

"Please, let's not." Hannah redirects the
conversation. "Did Jake call those people from
his firm? The security people."

"He did. They should be there soon. Did
something happen? What happened?"

Hannah starts to say something, then stops
herself. She thinks about telling her sister about
the guy in the laundry room. The knock at the

door. She can see Corny in her living room, pacing back and forth, worried beyond belief. Everything that's happened tonight stacked on top of the years of stress Hannah has brought down on her. Corny talked about the so-called limitless *gift card* of her help. Hannah can't help but feel that card is soaring past the limit Corny claims doesn't exist.

Everyone has a limit. Even sisters.

"Hannah? Why did you ask about the security from Jake's firm?"

Hannah squeezes the knife's handle tight. She's got this. Maybe not forever, but right now she knows what she needs to do. Focus on what she can control. She can stay in the apartment. Maybe let the cops do their jobs. But will they? Will they bend to the weight of the world begging them to tie this story to her no matter the truth? There are so many variables. So many spiderwebs of possibilities that all end with Hannah being dragged through complete hell, or ending up dead.

"What the hell can I control?" Her voice barely a whisper.

"Hannah?"

She closes her eyes, swallows hard.

"I'm fine. Just wanted to maybe try and get

some sleep. Thought maybe knowing there were beefy goons out there might help me relax some."

"Okay." Hannah can hear her sister exhale the breath she's probably been holding for an hour. "The relaxation goons are on the way. Try and get some rest."

"I'll try. Thank you again. I mean it."

Hannah taps the call away before her sister can.

She reaches for the Tito's, knowing damn well that she's hitting, or has slammed into, her booze limit for the evening. Problem is, she wants to crash through and make the world turn to dust. As she raises the bottle, she sees the card from Detective Huston. He said there might be questions later. Hates it but knows she might need contact him at some point.

She slides the card into the pocket stuck to the back of her phone.

Rolls her eyes as the booze burns. Then she stops, lowering the bottle.

Also on the counter is the card Alex Nord left in the laundry room. She'd set it next to her dad's envelope.

The card that says there's a lot she needs to know.

TEN

"Wow. Thought you'd call tomorrow, if at all, maybe even text first. But this works too."

Alex Nord had picked up on one ring.

Half a buzz probably.

Hannah had put the vodka away, but it had taken everything inside of her not to tilt the bottle back until her mind went blank as a sheet. She stares at the dark TV screen where the video of Zach played not long ago. She imagines it's running like a river nonstop throughout a world addicted to the twenty-four-seven news cycle. Something fresh for the unquenchable internet. Her heart thumps. She thinks of hanging up and running out of the building as fast as she can. She can cut through the crowd—

"Still there, Hannah? Last I checked, you called me."

"What do I need to know?"

"Pardon?"

"Your cute little note said I need to know things."

"Oh yeah. Sorry for being so... I don't know what. But in general, in a basic knowledge sense? Some say in today's world that math and science are the cornerstones, but I still feel, as I've always felt, reading and writing are the true—"

"Are you having fun?" Hannah realizes her voice is booming. Pulls it back. "You said there was a lot I needed to know. Start with who the hell are you."

"Okay. I'm a writer. Do some freelance reporting for various publications. Investigative reporting. Maybe you've seen my stuff."

"No." Hannah moves, picking around the room as if some new solution is hiding under the crap in her apartment. "So you did, what? Snuck into my building, hunted me down to... what exactly? Get the scoop? That your thing? Sell my story for a quick payday?"

"Not entirely. Although your story can and would fetch more than a few bucks right now. It's harder for those vultures to get into the building than one might think, but eventually they'll figure out a way to get to you. Or they'll just make shit up."

"How did you get in?"

"Well, that's the cool part." She can hear Nord take a swig of something. "I do live here."

Hannah can't help but snicker.

"Better to be lucky than good. But I have a washer and dryer, so I feel the social hierarchy of this place dictates that I be allowed to talk with you."

"Do you?" Hannah starts to pace. Now she really wants that drink.

"I do, but what I wrote on that card wasn't complete bullshit. There is a lot you don't know about this situation."

"Educate me quick or this conversation ends."

"In person. Don't like phones. We can start off the record if you like."

"Is that a joke?"

"No joke." Nord resets. "If I wanted to do something psycho, don't you think I would have done it in the laundry room?"

Hannah stops. Peeks out the window. Seems like the numbers outside are growing.

"Did you knock on my door?"

"What?"

"A few minutes ago, did you knock on my door?"

"No. Why would I—"

"Never mind."

Hannah pushes away the thought that someone else is out there roaming the halls waiting for her. Too terrifying to process right now. She rereads the card for the hundredth time.

There's a lot you need to know, Hannah.

"Where?"

"*Where* what?"

"Where will you be telling me what I need to know?"

"Well." Nord takes another swig, sounds like he's pacing too. "Going off campus—as it were— seems a little rough. Crowd is a little dense out there. Seems like only a matter of time before your apartment is a prime target for guests— meaning swarming reporters. How about my place?"

"Not a chance in hell."

"Fine. Fine. You're right. That was sort of creepy. Trust has hardly been established. Apologies. You name a place."

Hannah thinks. Moving to her closet, she

pulls out a workout bag, then moving to her bedroom, she begins stuffing various clothes inside. She's working on pure instinct, unsure of the right or wrong move to make. Nord is probably right. The building will do their best to keep people out, but the media is pretty good at worming their way into places they're not allowed. Each tick of the clock matters. She might be a sitting duck in her apartment. Corny said Jake's people would be there soon, but would they be there in time? Someone has already found her door.

"Still there, Hannah?"

"Hang on." Thinks. "Go to the deck upstairs."

"The party pool thing? It's partially closed. Doing some repairs, remodeling or something."

Hannah checks the time on her phone. It's little after six a.m. She remembers the emails from her building. The crews work on the remodel early in the morning during the week to maximize time so the tenants can enjoy the pool early evenings, nights, and weekends.

"Very good, Nord. It'll be you, me, and some contract maintenance crew guys who will gladly mind their own business unless I start screaming. A slimy, low-end, aging reporter like yourself should have zero problems hanging out in a *sort of* private place to chat with the most popular girl in town."

"Okay. Hurtful, but okay."

She shoves her father's envelope into the bag, along with the bottle of Tito's. Eyes the card from Detective Huston in the silicon pocket on the back of her phone. Hates the idea that she'll ever talk to them again.

"Here are my rules." She slips her knife into the bag as well. "You get one minute to keep me from walking away. If what you have to say is compelling, then I stay another minute. I stay until you're no longer helpful. Deal?"

There's a long pause.

"Nord?"

"Oh, I'm loving how you're pretending you have better, more amazing options."

"I've got options, you smug asshole."

"Do you? Do you have anyone in your orbit who truly knows anything about what's actually going on?"

"What?"

There's a soft knock at her door. Her heart all but stops. She reaches for the knife, gripping the handle inside her bag.

"I'll save you the time." Hannah can hear

Nord's voice outside the door. "It is me this time."

Hannah flings open the door, about to lay into him. Nord holds up a finger, stopping her before she can start.

"I'm the only source of real information you have in this ugly little world. What I know you can't find on a screen you have access to. You won't get this info chatting with whoever you chat with. So yeah, please, with some sugar, let's go hang out at the pool while they perform the semi-annual semen and urine scrub."

Hannah winces, knowing he's probably right. About the pool and other things. He's right about the low number people she knows who might have real information. Things she can't obtain by tapping at her phone or talking to Corny and her lawyer brother-in-law. Unsettling to think this Nord guy might be the only person who knows anything. Or he might not know anything at all.

Nord walks away from the doorway, vanishing into the hall.

Hannah peeks her head out. Nord stops, stares back as if waiting for a child to catch up. Hannah grabs her bag and locks the door behind her. Alex points to her door.

"Get your jacket. Chilly this time of the morning."

Hannah rolls her eyes, shows the jacket that's stuffed in her bag.

"Well, that's a good sign. If you packed, you're probably not thinking of killing yourself."

"Not the suicidal type."

"Excellent."

They move down the hall side by side, rushing but not running, neither looking to one another. Hannah checks behind them every few steps, scanning for whoever was at her door.

"I brought some wine." Nord taps the leather backpack thrown over his shoulder, then shoves open the door leading to the stairs.

"I brought some vodka."

"Wonderful. It's a real party now."

"And a big knife."

ELEVEN

THE WIND COMES AND GOES.

Quick bursts blast across the rooftop deck.

Gusts cut through Hannah, then the hard winds pull back into complete stillness. Not ideal up here by any stretch, but it is private except for the spattering of maintenance workers, and there's little chance anyone else will find her up here. She hopes. The pool is dark but the waterfall at the far end provides a nice rhythm that breaks up the quiet.

Nord hands her a glass of wine. A *glass* is being kind. He brought two red plastic Solo cups, as if this were a high school keg party. She waits for him to take a drink first. Watched him pour hers with a careful eye but still wanted to see him drink what came out of the bottle.

"Thanks." She takes a chug, then points at him. "Now. Talk."

Nord rolls his eyes, waiting for a better way to be asked.

"Really? Okay. Please, super-smart Alex Nord, tell me everything you know."

"Better. If we're going to work together, we need—"

"Work together?" She leans in. "No. No. You need to—"

"Too soon. Got it." He nods. Takes a drink. "The hyper cryptic *a lot you need to know* phrasing was unfortunate but necessary to get your attention. What's happening to you? What happened tonight with that loony barista? You're not the only one."

"What do you mean?" Hannah leans back, clutching her cup. "Zach's done this before?"

"No. Well, not that I know of. What I mean is, you're not the first woman who's had some guy she barely knows commit murder and then say he did it for them. And I don't mean in the bizarre *love triangle gone wrong* kind of way. This has happened before and in almost the same way it went tonight with you."

Hannah takes a drink. Nord pours her a bit more, then starts pulling items out from his bag.

"Who else?" Hannah asks, unsure she really wants to know. "How many times?"

"Three. You're the fourth as far as I know." Nord pulls out stacks of papers clipped together, along with his laptop. Opening the lid, he taps and types, then turns his screen around while scooting in closer to her. "Here. Julie McMahon. She was minding her own business when a waiter at her local sandwich shop killed two people in a parking lot, then turned himself in at a police station covered in blood saying he did it for Julie." He clicks and taps a few times, pulling up another file and dragging it next to the first. "This one, same thing. Except this guy worked at a grocery store and—"

Hannah's head starts spinning again.

Nord's voice fades into the background.

She sets down the wine. Her eyes bore through the screen, looking at the faces of the women. Pretty. Smiling. Look like nice people. Then Hannah looks at the pictures of the men. Average-looking guys. Not stunning, but not unattractive by any means. Guys you might know from anywhere. A boy you knew from high school. A man you passed on the way to work every day. Nothing about them that screams *Psycho! Stay away from these whackos.*

Much like Zach. These women probably talked to them on a regular basis. Part of the routine of their lives.

"What happened to them?" Hannah asks.

"To who?"

"These women. What happened to them after all this? I see the dates there. One was about three years ago, the others about two. Where are they now?"

Nord runs his tongue across his teeth. Struggling for a way to say it.

"Tell me."

"These two are dead. One to suicide."

Hannah swallows hard. "And the other?"

"She was killed. They didn't catch who did it."

Hannah feels her stomach drop, as if she were pushed off the building, her legs and arms flailing for stable ground. She springs up from her chair, grabbing her bag.

"Hannah, I know this is heavy stuff, but—"

"I'm gone."

"You can't simply run away. It's a freak show out there and they all want a piece of you."

Pushing past him, she storms fast toward the door that leads to the stairs, her bag thrown over her shoulder with the strap held tight in her fist.

Maybe the guys Jake got to guard the building are here now.

Maybe they're not.

Maybe they are held up somewhere. More important clients at Jake's firm have priority. Maybe they can't get here until later. She could call Corny again. *What do I say? Do I really want to pull Corny and her family further into this?* Deeper into the crazy.

Oh God, not Luna.

The ideas spin. Her mouth goes dry as her mind spirals down. New idea. Run like hell and never look back. She'll talk to the doorman. He'll know a discreet way out of the building. She can sneak out, slide away into the night. There must be a service entrance or maintenance exit through the garage or something. The doorman likes her. She gives him cookies and a Taco Deli gift card at Christmas.

"Hannah," Nord calls out.

Charging toward the exit, seconds planting her palm on the metal and shoving it open, Hannah can almost feel the relief from breaking free of this insanity.

"The third one is still alive."

Hannah stops, turns back to him.

Nord rises to his feet, framed under the

moonlight. Her jaw tightens. Two of the maintenance workers turn, looking to Hannah. She puts
up a hand letting them know it's okay.

"I know where she is. She's not easy to find,
mind you." Nord steps cautiously toward her.
"Been off the grid ever since. She turned herself
into a ghost. Simply vanished from the planet.
But I found her." He waves his hands, circling
and crisscrossing along with his words. "There's a
pattern to these men. These murders. On the
surface it seems random, but it is not. Not when
you really look at them. This third woman—
Sloane is what she's going by these days—might
know something that can help you."

"Cool. Tell her I said *hey*."

"Hannah, this isn't going to go away.
Running won't stop it."

"I'll take my chances."

"This is going to happen to another woman.
Maybe a lot more. That what you want?"

Hannah clenches her fist. Can't believe he's
playing that card.

"Think about it. Sure, you could bolt. Run
like the wind. Understandable. Pretty scary stuff
to deal with. But maybe, just maybe, you could
play a part in stopping it from happening again."

"I didn't ask for this. I met a guy. I drank

some coffee..." Her words fade along with her focus. Struggles to find a clear thought. "I was taking a fucking bubble bath."

"I get it. I do. You didn't request any of this. But make no mistake... this is upon you."

Hannah locks eyes with his. He nods. She turns and walks away.

She hears him say things behind her. His words morph and muffle as she picks up her pace, sprinting by the time she reaches the stairs. Takes two, three at a time, almost flying down past floor after floor. She'll stop by her place and make sure she has everything—maybe she can stuff a couple more things in her bag—then she'll sweet-talk the doorman to let her out the unknown side door she's sure is there.

She can slip into the dark. Crash somewhere tonight, then maybe things will quiet down. The world will move on. Things will become normal.

Right? Maybe?

When it's safe, she can go to Corny's place for a few days to even out. All the horrible out there can find some other woman to traumatize.

Those other women aren't her problem.

A pang of guilt hits her for even thinking like that, but she can't save the world. She can barely take care of herself. What happened to them is done. As heartbreaking as it is, there's nothing she can do about it.

She won't let what happened to them land on top of her. The police will catch Zach and this will all be over soon enough. Hell, she might even go back to that therapist after it's all over. Sounds like a smart way to go, considering it feels like her mind is about to slide out of her ears and crawl away from her.

Slamming into the stairwell door, she pushes her way out onto the floor of her apartment. Fights to find her breath. Adjusts her bag.

Her feet skid to a stop. She holds on to the wall by her fingertips.

The door to her apartment is open wide.

Looks to be smashed in, wood splintered along the side. Hannah stands frozen in the hall-way. No idea what to do.

Someone is in there.

She can see a large shadow moving inside. A massive man moves past the open door. Hannah's heart thumps. He's easily six foot plus. Wide shoulders. She can hear him searching through her living room. Items hit the floor. He moves on, now rummaging through a drawer in the kitchen.

Is this the person who knocked before Nord?

Is this the guards Jake talked about? He didn't

say anything about them coming into her apartment.

Zach? Is he that big? No.

Her hand inches inside her bag, feeling the knife's handle. She thinks about running past the door, down to the elevator. She could make it, but if whoever is in there comes out, she'd be cut off. They'd block the way to the stairs, and she'd be left with only the elevator as her escape. She'd have to press the button and wait. Roll the dice on where the elevator car is located.

Hell no, her mind screams.

She takes two steps backward. The obvious pieces of logic start to click in place. Whoever is in there knows where she lives. Reporters wouldn't smash in the door and start ransacking her place like this. Cops would just have the building's management grab a key and open her place up. She watches the shadow move, holding her breath, watching to see if this person is coming out into the hallway. Hannah inches her way back toward the stairs, hand gripped tight around the knife, moving with as much silence as she can muster.

Her phone goes off. Buzzing. Rattling inside her bag. Her eyes pop wide.

The shadow stops moving. Paused and listening.

Hannah spins around, running with everything she has through the door to the stairs. She crashes into Nord, slamming them both into the brick wall of the stairwell.

"What the hell?" Nord grunts, bouncing off the bricks.

Hannah grabs him by the arm, pulling him along as she races down the stairs. Nord struggles to keep up but he's with her.

"Question?" Nord gets out between breaths.

"Later."

They hit the door that leads out into the subterranean parking area. Hannah jams her bag at the keypad. The fob on her keychain doesn't read. Light still glows red. She tries again. The door gives a soft beep, light goes green. They explode into the parking lot. A steel gate on the opposite side of the garage leads out into the city. Not lit great but there are lights that poke modest holes in the dark.

"Stop." Nord's lungs are obviously begging for air. "Talk to me."

"Someone was in my apartment."

"Okay." He looks back toward the door, then to a gray 4Runner. "Okay. I've got a car just over there." He pulls his keys out, pressing the unlock. "We can slip out. You can hide in the back so the freaks don't see you."

Hannah's head spins. *Am I really doing this? Is any of this really happening?*

"I'm going to ask some questions," she says, locking into his eyes. "Need you to skip past the bullshit."

"Fair enough." Nord motions for her to move toward his 4Runner.

"Do you really think they are all connected?" Hannah moves quick along with him. "Those women. Me."

"With all my heart."

Nord presses the button to open the hatch. Extends an inviting hand for her to lie down in the back. Hannah can't help but realize how crazy this is. She looks back to the building door.

"Why are you doing this? What's in it for you?"

Nord starts to speak. Hannah holds up a finger, letting him know that lies will not be tolerated. With a nod and a resetting pause, Nord's face loses its ever-present charm, slipping into a serious stare.

"I've been paid to write a book about what's happened. I'm way overdue on delivering. My publisher either wants the advance returned in full or the book. Part my fault. Other part is the world not cooperating. But then you happened." Big smile. "And here we are."

"And you're broke."

"As hell."

The door to the stairs starts to shake and rattle. Someone is trying to get through without a key card.

Nord gives Hannah a *now or never* look.

"Shit." Hannah crawls into the back of the 4Runner.

TWELVE

"You FAMILIAR WITH the phrase *final girl?*" Nord asks, playing with the radio.

Hannah stares out the window as the morning sun continues its rise, the beginnings of purple bruising smeared across the Texas sky that stretches across the universe. She can feel the cold of the air through the window. She works to keep herself awake, the events of the day taking a toll. The shots of Tito's and wine with Nord aren't helping either.

They'd stopped in a neighborhood that had dark streets so she could get out of the back. Didn't want to run the risk of stopping at some gas station and having video footage off a security camera getting leaked by an employee who wanted a moment of fame. Or worse, some half-wit customer pumping gas with a phone at the ready wanting to contribute footage to the scroll.

Nord has been playing an 80's playlist for hours. Hannah was into it for a while, but it's starting to grate her nerves now.

That, and she knows Nord is holding back information from her.

They've been driving for hours, heading west to a place Nord won't reveal. Going to where he thinks one of the women is currently living. Hiding is more accurate. Besides Hannah, this woman is the only one still alive.

This survivor known now as Sloane Franks.

According to Nord, she removed herself from the proverbial grid and has stayed off since the incident. There's nothing out there on the internet about Sloane Franks. At least nothing that would match the age and description of their Sloane. Nord told her Sloane's real name, and there's a couple of interviews here and there from right after the incident. Really only one of note. The second interview she ended abruptly and walked off in the middle of it. Just bolted off the television set, leaving an opened-mouthed TV personality, and she hasn't been seen since.

Now she's only a ghost story told by Nord.

"Final girl?" Hannah sips her truck stop

coffee, trying hard not to be a snob about how much it sucks. "I think so. Maybe. Books and movies, right? Something about serial killers or whatever."

"You're on the right track." Nord turns down The Cure. "You know how in all those slasher movies there's usually a huge body count at the hands of a chainsaw killer or a big boy with a machete and a hockey mask or whatever?"

Hannah nods.

"And at the end, there's usually one girl who's still alive running around and she takes out the madman."

"Sure. So what?"

"That's what they call Sloane." Nord looks over to Hannah as a check-in to see that she's paying attention. "She's a final girl."

"You said she went through what I'm going through."

"She did, but slightly different." Nord clears his throat, regrips the steering wheel. "Sloane was at a company retreat-style thing. Her firm paid for this team-building event out in the woods. Log cabins by a lake, like a summer camp sort of deal. Management and employees doing activities to build trust, bonding and all that horseshit. You know what I'm talking about?"

"Yeah, I'm familiar with corporate retreats." Hannah rubs her temple. "What the hell does this have to with me?"

Nord gets quiet for a second. Fiddles with the heat. Turns off The Cure.

He finally starts up again telling her about the company retreat, but also talks about how Sloane caught the eye of a young guy in the mailroom months before. He was just out of high school. Big, rugged good looks, dark hair, and crystal-blue eyes. But as women, including Sloane, spent more time around the mailroom, they started to notice something was off with this guy.

Seemed okay on the surface, but when you talked to him, you could see something about him —something to avoid.

There was darkness in his eyes. He'd hold his stare too long. The words he chose were odd. The things he said seemed strange, some of the women said later. He never did anything that would raise HR red flags, but there was just enough to cause a blip on the radar of most women. Some of the women referred to him as the *Creepy Hot Mailroom Guy*. Sloane was nice to him, maybe even flirted with him early on. But this guy—Logan Burke—took a shine to Sloane. A quiet obsession. So one night, he shows up at this corporate bonding event out in the woods.

Only he wasn't invited.

Hannah stares at Nord, knowing what's next. She pinches the skin on the top of her hand. Didn't even realize she was doing it. She returns her stare to the world outside the window, hoping the end of this story is somehow happy.

It's not. Not even close.

Logan showed up to the retreat wearing a sack over his head. A potato sack or something like it. Police think he stole it from a nearby farm where they found several mutilated animals. Logan cut slits in the sack for his blue eyes to burn through. There was another slit cut, one for his mouth. He carried an axe in his thick hands and had a rather large knife strapped to his tree stump of a leg.

Hannah closes her eyes. Leans her head on the window in the hopes the cool glass will ease the furnace that's burning inside her.

Logan slipped out of the woods on that night. Everyone was sitting in a circle around a big, crackling fire. There was wine. Good food. Employees were laughing, unwinding with the aid of the wine and sharing stories of corporate unfairness.

A father of three who was sitting next to Sloane was the first to be killed.

Logan planted his axe into the man's neck. Sloane was sprayed, covered in blood. The running began. Screams started to echo through the woods. Logan wasted no time. He hacked and grabbed, cutting through bodies that were too terrified to move. A brutal model of murder efficiency. Fast and strong, pausing only long enough to watch one of the bodies burn in the fire. As if admiring his work.

Frantic calls to 911 went out, and the police got there as soon as they could. But this was a small town in the mountains with twisty, winding, one-lane roads. And in a horrible event like this, seconds mattered. Minutes were like an eternity.

Sloane helped coworkers to their feet, only to see them chopped down, slipping away from her blood-slick hands. Logan could have easily killed Sloane many times. Multiple opportunities to cut her to pieces if that's what he wanted. It wasn't. It became clear he was only there for her. He was showing off for her. As if he thought the killing would let her know how much he cared for her.

Hoping she would connect the dots, read between the lines of his slaughter.

Sloane fell in the dirt, somehow got to her feet. Scrambling, she made it into where the dining room and the kitchen of the camp were located. She knew she had to find a weapon. She flung the drawers open and found a butcher knife. Not a violent person at all, she hoped she would have it in her to use it. All the while, she prayed the police would show up and put an end to the nightmare, even though she knew it was a long shot.

Logan stormed into the kitchen. Without hesitation, Sloane jammed the knife into his ribs. He grunted but barely flinched. He backhanded her into the wall, muttering something about *connecting the dots* and nonsense about *what's between the words can save us or slaughter us.*

She clawed at his head trying to rip the sack free. She landed punches anywhere she could. Put a knee to his balls, thumbs in his eyes. But he held on tight to her through it all, driven beyond pain and reason. Logan slammed her against the wall over and over, just shy of knocking her unconscious. Her mind turned to fuzz. Vision all but gone.

Logan worked his mouth through the slit he'd cut in the sack, then sunk his teeth deep into Sloane's shoulder, drawing blood like an animal.

Dropping the axe, holding her with both hands, he bit into her again and again. In the police report, Sloane stated she could hear him make a sound. Like a satisfied baby.

Her vision slipped, threads of consciousness unraveling.

Through the fog, she felt his grip loosen ever so slightly. Presumably the joy he experienced from the taste of her, the thrill, made him lose some of his intense focus. She pushed off him enough to create some space, spinning herself free onto the floor.

As Logan whipped around, Sloane grabbed the axe, swinging with everything she had left.

"He killed everyone at the retreat except for Sloane. She fought like hell, got beaten up bad. Some pretty ugly wounds. Just shy of a serious head injury, but she managed to land that axe right into the middle of his chest. That's when the cops showed up. Sloane stood there in the kitchen, a broken mess. Logan dropped down to his knees and said he did it—"

"For her." Slips out barely above a whisper.

Nord snaps his fingers, pointing a *you got it, kid* her way.

"I remember hearing about that, the mass murder at a corporate retreat. But I never heard about the killer saying that, that it was about a woman."

"That's because it never got out. Not to the mainstream media at least."

"So how do you know?"

"I just know."

Hannah entertains the idea of opening the door and rolling out into the countryside. She'd had a chance to run at her apartment. She should have taken the opportunity when she had it.

The weight of this crashes down on her. She needs to talk to Corny. Her sister will have no idea what to do—who would?—but there's comfort in her voice. A feeling of home when Corny tries to apply logic to things that defy it. Like their dad leaving them. Like Mom shutting down. Like psychopaths killing people for you.

The question rolls through her mind. *Do I want to make my sister part of this?*

She'll talk to her, of course she will, but to what end? Keeping Corny away keeps Luna out of this too.

"Any who." Nord turns the '80s back on. Tears for Fears is up. "That's the story of why Sloane is called a final girl."

Hannah clears her throat. Pushes the fear down. She needs to find her best impression of a badass no matter how much she wants to turn into a puddle.

Hannah turns the music back down. "Woman."

"What?"

"It should be final woman. They should be final women, not final girls. It's dismissive."

"Okay. Sure. I get that. But the known phrase is final girl, not final woman."

"Don't give a damn what the socially accepted phrase is."

"Final women sounds like the sequel to *Little Women*."

"I do love that book."

"The movie too."

"Oh yeah. The movie's good as hell, yes."

Only the sounds of the road fill the car. Tires gripping the asphalt. Rushing roar of wind hitting the car, then splitting off on a different path. Winds of West Texas can be pretty strong. Not much to stop them out here. Flat land. Few trees, if any, to slow the rush and not much in the way of man-made structures to hold them back either. An oil derrick pumps in the distance. Hannah watches its relentless search into the ground. The sun is gaining more airspace by the minute.

"Have you met Sloane before?"

"Me?" Nord fidgets with the collar of his shirt.

"Who else would I be talking about?"

"We've met."

"Oh. *You've met?* You were just going to leave it at that."

"I was."

Hannah presses her lips together. No strength left to fight for this line of questioning.

"We'll grab a couple of rooms at this dump a few miles from here. It's just outside Odessa. Try and grab an hour or two of sleep. Recharge a bit, then go to where I think she is."

"*Think* she is."

"She isn't expecting visitors. And yes, sorry, I'm not completely sure she's there. She's fairly nimble with her domiciles. Think I brought that up."

"You didn't."

"Oh, thought I did. Well, I should have."

"Yeah, seems like you should have mentioned a lot of shit."

"When we get there, you should let me talk to her. Chances are good there might be some early tension. Maybe some hurt feelings but..."

He waves off his own notion of *hurt* and *tension*. "It'll be fine."

Hannah holds her stare.

Nord refuses to look her way, turning Tears for Fears back up.

Not a chance in hell this will be fine.

"Just so I'm clear." Nord clears his throat. "I can say final *girl?*"

"I don't give a shit."

Hannah changes the station to some classic rock.

Stevie Nicks fills the space between them.

THIRTEEN

Breakfast was quiet.

Nord, for first time in their twisted relationship, had been rendered speechless.

Seemed to have been lost in his own thoughts ever since Hannah sat down. He managed to offer a *good morning* but that was about it. Suited her just fine. "Angel of the Morning" was playing overhead anyway.

Hannah devoured the bacon and eggs special and still wanted three more plates of it. She chugs the diner coffee as if the meaning of life were carved into the bottom of the somewhat clean mug. The radiant sun shreds through the place, cutting the floors and walls into thick slots through the cheap blinds.

Outside, it's eighty-two in the sun. Fifty-one

in the shade. Winds gusting up to thirty mph. West Texas winterish weather. Might snow. Might not. Keep on living and keep your complaints to yourself.

Hannah is pretty sure she's seen Nord's lips move a couple of times. Working through some sort of mental puzzle. Upon second look, it's more like he's practicing lines. Running through the conversation he's going to have with Sloane, no doubt.

Hannah has been watching him for a long time. Leaning back into the red vinyl booth, sipping her surprisingly good coffee, picking away at her side order of bacon, an add-on to the bacon on her original plate, all while studying Nord. She even swiped a piece off his plate to see how deep in thought he truly was. He didn't notice at all, or at least he didn't say anything. That's how far back into his own head he was.

There's a history between these two. Hannah can tell that much.

A heavy piece of history being lugged around by Nord. What does Final Girl Sloane have over him? Something Nord is more than a little concerned about. He mutters something soft and low, writes something down on a paper napkin, then wads the napkin up, seemingly disgusted with himself.

Hannah has let this go as long as she can.

"Money or sex?" she asks.

Nord almost chokes on his own tongue.

"One more time?"

"Is it about money or sex?" Hannah leans in. "You and Sloane. That's the only two things that could make a dude like you so damn nervous about seeing her again. Good God look at you, man."

Nord motions for the check.

"Which is it, Nord?"

"I'm not answering that."

"I'm going to find out. We're headed her way as soon as you pick up the tab."

"Thought we might split the bill."

"Do you want me to ask her? Because I can."

"No need to—"

"*Hey, Sloane, what's the deal between you and Shakespeare here?*"

Nord slams his hands on the table.

Mugs jump, spilling dollops of coffee. His charm and wit gone. His cool exterior just revealed a major crack. This immediate, hard-hitting shift in personality is a side to Nord

Hannah has not seen. One she isn't enjoying. She cocks her head, gripping her fork.

In this moment, it is crystal clear she doesn't know this guy. Not really. Something she already knew, but she wasn't expecting the sudden change in the little writer from the laundry room.

Things had moved so fast last night. The apartment. The large man searching her place. The people outside the building all wanting a piece of her. During all of it, Nord was a calm voice. He had information. He made sense.

Was he just telling me what I wanted to hear?

A comforting port of safety in a raging storm. Someone saying they wanted to help her, that they had some answers to all her impossible questions. Were all of his words and banter to lure her out into the wilds of West Texas? His stories about mass murder at corporate retreats and final girls. All while taking her somewhere, not giving her the details as to where.

"I'm sorry." Nord's face hangs off his skull. "It's the zero sleep. Too much coffee. A lot has happened. I'm a little off." He pauses. Restarts. "There are stresses, right? Things happen. Choices made. I know there's a mountain of stress on you too—not suggesting there's not—but

I've got an unhealthy helping of stress served up to me as well."

The check arrives.

He locks with her eyes, waiting for a confirmation that they're cool. Nord must be picking up on her concern. A flimsy trust in him that's fading by the second. Perhaps the fork she's holding as a weapon was his first clue.

She holds his stare. Tries to read his eyes.

Her skill in reading people has been less than perfect over the years. She knows it all too well. She also knows she doesn't have a ton of great options right now. One thing for sure, she'll keep one hand on that knife in her bag the rest of the trip.

"Okay," she finally says.

Nord carefully counts out the bills. Hannah can see what he's leaving barely covers the tab.

"I promise you'll find out everything about Sloane and me soon enough," Nord says as he slides out from the booth with his laptop bag in hand. "Then you can make a judgment. Fair?"

"Fair enough."

Hannah tosses a generous tip onto the table as she watches him walk toward the door.

FOURTEEN

FEELS like they've been driving for days.

Hannah knows it's been more like an hour or two, but still.

Plodding along the desert-like land of West Texas can seem at times as if you're not really moving. There's a special kind of beauty to it, however, Hannah thinks. Didn't believe that at first, but the land is growing on her. The simplicity of it. There's an odd sense of security out here. She gets why Sloane picked this area to get lost in. They haven't seen more than one eighteen-wheeler and two Ford F-150s for miles. After what Sloane has been through, a deep desire for isolation is understandable.

Hannah feels restless. They've been on this dirt road for a while.

The jarring bumps and holes have her longing for the smooth, open highways they've enjoyed up until now. She so badly wants to ask *are we there yet* but knows this is not the time or place. Her fingertips press into the 4Runner's leather seats. She could hold on to the *oh shit* handle by the window but doesn't want Nord to see her anxiety spiking.

Nord has his hands planted firmly at ten and two. His body leans in close to the wheel, his shoulders up high like earrings. He glances at his phone occasionally. Moves his fingers flipping between things, pausing to enlarge an image. Hannah assumes there's a map of some sort on the glass he's working over. At times it looks like his eyes could pop out of his head. Between the phone and the windshield, he's straining his eyes so hard to find something out there among the dirt, brush and hills. Hasn't even bothered to turn on the '80s jams.

Hannah keeps her bag in her lap. Unzipped just enough so she can see the knife.

She's made the mental reps of how she'd snatch and pull it free if she needs to. Even adjusted it strategically while Nord wasn't looking. Her fingers touch the knife's handle every so often for comfort.

Nord takes his foot off the gas.

Hannah's body jolts forward, bounces as they hit a hole in the dirt.

"There," he says, pointing in the distance like a child who's spotted Santa.

Nord stomps on the brakes.

It's hard to see through the cloud of dust the 4Runner's sudden stop has formed. Taking a beat, Hannah waits for the dust to clear. Adjusting the cheap sunglasses she picked up at the diner, she tries to see out in the distance despite the raging sun.

"I don't see anything."

"Up there." Nord's excitement has him almost hopping out of his seat. "Along the bottom of the hill. It's in the shade, but you can see the metal box-looking things."

Hannah squints hard, following his outstretched finger toward the hill. There is something that shines as the clouds drift past. A ray of light bounces off a piece of metal, then the light is muted quick by the rolling, returning clouds.

As her eyes adjust, she zeroes in, can barely make out what Nord is talking about. Nord takes his foot off the brake, letting the 4Runner slow-roll forward. With every foot they crawl closer, Hannah can make out a little more.

Doesn't look like much, but up ahead is a metal shack of some kind. A home pieced together with what looks like steel shipping containers but done with purpose.

There's a front door made of glass, or perhaps clear plastic, with a well-crafted small wood deck with a faded red rocking chair. The roof is metal sheets with solar panels along the top. Large stones have been stacked, piled up around the home, creating a knee-high wall. Possibly to deter unwanted critters, Hannah thinks. To the left is what seems to be a shower/bathroom maybe, and to the left of that is a smaller metal shed with more solar panels and water tanks attached with white PVC piping.

"You been out here before?" Hannah asks.

"No. Following a strong lead." He cracks a smile. "She's been busy. Resourceful as hell."

Hannah sees the front bumper of what looks like an older truck parked behind the home.

"Oh." Hannah is now the one pointing. "She's got a pet."

The full-blown Texas longhorn moves casually through what one could generously call the front yard. The span of the cow's horns is impressive. The majestic beast looks up from searching the dirt, staring directly at them.

"I think we've been made." Hannah feels a knot form in her stomach, although she's not sure why. "Do they charge cars or anything?"

"Hope not."

Hannah looks around. Open land as far as the eye can see save for the hill behind the home. Looks steep. Not a mountain or anything, but easily a few stories tall. Few places for bad guys to hide. That's why this is perfect for Sloane. Any potential threat would have to either move across miles of open, flat land or try to scale a steep, multi-story hill and come over the top. As long as she's paying attention, there's not much chance of someone sneaking up on her. Not impossible but the odds are in her favor at least.

"Smart," Hannah mutters to herself.

"Well, we're all in now." Nord swallows hard and rubs a scar under his chin.

Hannah hadn't noticed it before; his morning stubble makes it stand out. Nord is visibly on edge as they roll toward the home. She can see his jaw clench. They are still about fifty yards away, but Nord is closing the distance at a slow and steady pace.

"Let me do the talking."

"Yeah." Hannah checks her knife again. "You said that."

There's no movement around the house. Impossible to tell what's going on inside. The door remains closed. Makeshift curtains cover the window. The outdoor bathroom seems to be empty. Even the longhorn doesn't seem to be too disturbed by the new visitors.

Nord slips the 4Runner into park, takes a deep breath, looks to Hannah with bouncing eyes, then fumbles to open the door.

Hannah looks to her bag.

Do I bring it with me? Will that just put Sloane more on edge?

Hannah doesn't feel great about strolling in without something in hand, but she also doesn't want to set this woman off either. Decides to split the difference. She leaves the bag in the passenger seat, unzipped for easy access to the knife, with the 4Runner's door unlocked. At least she'll have a place to run to if things get weird out here.

Scratch that. Weirder.

Their footsteps crunch into the hard dirt and small rocks. Nord seems to be watching the ground as well as the area in front of him. Up and down, then side to side. Like he's anticipating the worst from any and all possible angles. Keeps rubbing the scar on his chin.

A cool wind blows, cutting the sun's warming light. Nord stops a few feet from the deck of the home and holds his hand up, signaling for Hannah to stop. Seconds beat like a hammer. The wind cuts through her. Her heart thumps the most primal rhythm Hannah has ever known.

A shotgun pumps.

"Hands up and empty," a woman says.

Nord sets down his bag slow and careful. Hannah raises her arms up as if she were in a movie bank robbery. A tumbleweed rolls past the longhorn. As they both turn, they find a Mossberg 12-gauge pointed in the general direction of their faces.

The woman looks as if she's carved out of stone.

Her triceps pop while holding the shotgun tight to her shoulder. Sweat gives a shine to the tangle of thorns-and-roses tattoos that line her left arm from wrist to shoulder blade. Reminds Hannah of a meaner version of the woman who teaches classes at the gym down the street from her building.

"What do you want, Nord?" Sloane asks. Her voice is raspy and done with bullshit.

"Love it if you lowered that cannon."

Sloane wraps the shotgun over her shoulder by its sling, then pulls a handgun from behind her back, letting it hang by her side with her finger just off the trigger. Her eyebrows rise. *Now what?*

"This is Hannah Rush," Nord says. "She's been—"

"I know who she is." Sloane takes a step forward. "Internet is surprisingly okay out here."

"Nice. Thought you might... ya know." Nord looks back behind him at the shipping container condo. "Thought you might have a nicer place. No offense. But considering the money you took from—"

"Careful, Nord." Sloane takes another step closer. Hannah can see herself and Nord in the reflection of Sloane's sunglasses. "Choose what you say next very carefully."

The longhorn strolls past. Hannah fights to not to jump, but her body still gives a jolt.

"Waylon there won't hurt you, Hannah. He's good people."

Hannah wants to fire off questions like a machine gun but stops herself.

What she would really love to do is tear open that hole in the universe she's been fantasizing about and hide inside. But that's not realistic. Instead, she'll have to settle for this unfolding drama playing out between these two characters. Pretend she's a member of the audience instead of part of the cast.

"So?" Sloane motions for them to lower their hands. "How did you find me?"

"Kind of what I do for a living."

"Been kind of shitty at it."

"With little help from you."

"Well, if you haven't heard, I'm an emotionally stunted final girl."

Hannah isn't sure if she's impressed with Sloane's self-awareness or horrified at how all this has made her colder than cold.

Is this what the world has done to her? What was she like before?

Nord said she worked for a company, in an office, just like Hannah. She looks over Sloane. Her short, jet-black hair is pulled back in a small, tight ponytail. She's obliviously cut and dyed it not long ago. Must change her look when she changes addresses.

Is this the life that waits for me?

"I was just starting to make this a real home, Nord." Sloane's eyes look past him. "Made all this with my own two hands. Kinda proud of it, actually. Thought I might be here for a minute. Put down some roots."

"Just you and Waylon in the wild, wild West. Quite a life you've carved out for yourself."

Sloane adjusts her grip on the gun.

Hannah is sure she's going to shoot him between the eyes.

"You could have found a more stable living arrangement," Nord says. "That's what I was trying to help you to do."

Sloane moves in on Nord in a blink. An inch from his face.

"You were trying to own my story. Eat it up, shit it out, then serve it to the world. Big book tour. Make the morning talk show circuit. Movie deals. Limited series, they call them. Documentary, maybe. All while I'm the wounded animal of the moment."

Nord shifts his feet. Avoids eye contact.

"What happened?" Hannah's voice cracks. She couldn't wait any more. "What did Nord do?"

"Well, Hannah Rush." Sloane takes a step back away from Nord. "Your buddy here got a huge advance to write about me and some other women who had a similar experience." Her eyes light up, pointing to Hannah. "You know, oddly enough, it's not unlike the drama you're wrapped up in currently. Funny how that works."

Hannah looks to Nord. At least he's been telling her a version of the truth.

"He convinced an agent, then a media company with a publishing wing along with streaming and film production, that he'd uncovered a connection between all of us. A through line of a story that even the most passive of true crime enthusiasts would devour. Eyes, ears, and souls."

"I tried to find a way for all of us to benefit from something unfortunate."

"But no one more than you, right?" Sloane taps her gun by her side. "So, he reached out to me. Gave me a few bucks to—"

"A few?" Nord pipes up. "That what we're calling it now?"

"You really want to put a price tag on it?" Sloane rips off her sunglasses. Searing eyes rival the punishing sun. "He paid me nickels and dimes compared to his paycheck. I've heard about unequal pay, but good God, man. His loose change in exchange for my story. For my pain. So, with a song in my heart, I took his scraps and left. Not proud of it, nor am I ashamed."

Hannah looks Nord over.

His vacant stare out into the dirt looks as if his mortal soul has skipped town. Sloane slips her gun behind her back while inching closer to Nord.

"I'm guessing he's up against it, and if snarky little Nord here doesn't produce something soon, he'll have to pay back that big, fat advance. Heard it was what? North of seven figures? Streaming deals, podcast could push it higher." Sloane claps her hands an inch from his nose. Nord jumps, snapping out of his trance. "Guessing your dumb ass burned through all that money."

Nord's eyes tell Hannah how right Sloane is.

"Did it again, Nord? Sad. Thought you were a writer. A seeker of truth." Sloane turns to Hannah. "Cocaine and hookers. He's got a history of weakness with those two specific itches."

"I'm a child of the eighties." Nord holds his arms out wide. "Sue me."

"But the good Lord shined upon you, right? Somehow, some way, something came along that might just bail out your sorry ass." Sloane is enjoying this a little too much. She points to Hannah. "You happened, sweet darling."

Nord turns with his back to them, walking toward the steel shack. Hannah tries to stop him.

"Let him go." Sloane casually slips her gun from behind her back, letting it sway by her side once again. "But stay out of my house, Nord. Bathroom is over there if that's an immediate need."

A twig snaps behind Sloane.

She whips around with her gun leveled.

A large man stands behind Sloane, his gun already on her.

Hannah can barely see a dark-blue sedan parked in the distance, much farther back from Nord's 4Runner. Hannah knows that she and Nord caused Sloane to lose focus. No way this guy would ever get the jump on her under normal circumstances.

The large man's black T-shirt strains to contain his arms. Biceps big as thighs. His bald head glistens under the relentless sun. Hannah looks him over. There's a strange familiarity but she can't place it.

The large man looks to Hannah, then to Nord. "You okay?"

Sloane's eyes dart to her, then back to the man. "This beast a friend of yours?"

Hannah looks to Nord, who shrugs. Hannah

turns her attention back to the large man. Can't place him. Then her mind clicks in place. Her apartment.

"Were you..." Hannah moves closer. "Were you in my apartment last night?"

The man takes his eyes off Sloane, but for only a moment.

"Yes."

"Find what you were looking for?"

"I was hired to—" The large man takes a step forward as he tries to explain.

Wrong choice.

Sloane is on him in a snap.

Her speed is jaw-dropping. Pushing Hannah aside, she plants a foot to the man's knee. As the knee snaps, she jams her shoulder under his meaty forearm. His gun arm pumps up, aiming harmlessly at the sky. A lightning-quick chop to the throat, followed by a pop of his elbow, drops both the man's gun and body to the dirt, leaving him fighting to find air.

Hannah picks up his gun.

She's neither a gun person nor an anti-gun person, but she has fired a weapon before. She and her sister lived together briefly after Hannah graduated college and while Corny was engaged, and they decided they should have some protection in their tiny apartment. They went to a class together, learned enough to get comfortable keeping a low-end Sig secured in a safe in the hall closet. Fortunately, she'd never had a reason to remove it from the metal box, let alone use it.

All that *training* has long left her mind, but Hannah still has some of the main points scattered in the corners of her memory. She holds the gun with both hands, feet shoulder width apart, knees slightly bent, puts the large man in her sights.

"Who are you?" she asks, gun shaking slightly.

Sloane steps back beside Hannah, keeping her gun on him as well. She scans the area, looking to see if he has any friends.

The surrounding land looks as barren as it did before. Hannah thinks how Sloane cannot be happy about all the excitement that's shown up at her home today.

Nord seems oddly quiet. Almost removing himself from the situation.

The man winces, holding his knee while trying to get up. "I was hired to find you, Hannah."

FIFTEEN

"Okay. What were you hired to do when you found me?" Hannah's anger rolls.

Is he with the police? Worse?

"Provide personal protection."

"Bullshit." Hannah can't match her false bravado with her expression. Tough-kid words delivered with the look of a child who wants to hide under the bed.

"I can prove it." He glances to his pocket with *may I?* eyes.

"Absolutely not." Sloane steps closer. Gun leveled on his skull.

Hannah's mind flashes to her brother-in-law telling her his firm would send someone. Strains to remember the exact words he used, but he said something about sending someone to watch her apartment. Her sister had verified they were on their way.

But how did he find me out here in the middle of nowhere?

Was he following us the whole time? All the way from downtown Austin?

Possible, but that level of dedication to the job seems rare.

"Let's get inside." Sloane's still scanning the area as she moves behind the man, keeping her gun on him. "Just in case shit gets shittier. Oh yeah," stabbing her eyes at Hannah. "Give me that gun, gorgeous."

Hannah almost hands it to her but realizes that would be dumb as hell.

"No thank you," she says.

"Like me to take it from you?"

"That's what you're going to have to do." They both step up onto the wood deck. "I don't trust you and you don't trust me. Fine. I get that. But I'd like to keep this as fair as possible."

Sloane offers nothing, juts her chin toward the door.

As they enter, Nord stays quiet. Keeps his head down.

Hannah can't help but marvel at Sloane's place. First, it's bigger than she expected. Not huge by any stretch of the imagination, but not the tiny box she thought it was from the outside. There's a certain unexpected charm to the place. Far from the Four Seasons but not horrible.

Some of the walls are painted in a soothing shade of blue, while others are wood with the container's steel walls peeking through. There are paintings hanging in what could best be described as a master bedroom, and the kitchen would make many New York apartment dwellers jealous. A minimalist's wonderland with some nice touches to make it home.

"Pretty sure this guy was hired by someone I know," Hannah says, looking the place over. "Jake call you?"

The man keeps quiet, neither confirming nor denying.

"Well, if it's all the same to everyone," Sloane says as she moves inside, "I'll keep my trust on hold." She reaches in a drawer, removes some zip ties, then secures the large man's hands. With a nudge of her gun, she positions him with his back against the wall just right of the open door.

Hannah takes in the rest of Sloane's home. There's a collection of tactical knives that might seem randomly scattered around at first glance. One on a bedside table. Two others hang on alternate walls in the kitchen. They are all a few steps away from one another.

Grab-and-go blades.

Sloane moves a rifle with a high-powered scope away from the door. Safe distance from the large man. Another handgun—looks a lot like the Sig she and her sister had—sits on a small kitchen table. Looks like Sloane was cleaning it. Another shotgun rests near a very used punching bag that hangs off to the side of the main room. There are dumbbells and a jump rope on a padded floor mat that's torn at the edges. Explains how Sloane got the arms Hannah would die for.

Out here alone in the desert training. Ready for anything or anyone.

A laptop sits on a desk crafted from a door and some cinder blocks. A yellow legal pad sits next to it with what looks like pages of hand-scribbled notes. Black and red pens ready for her to capture her thoughts.

Hannah saw the way Sloane handled her gun. The way she took this guy down in a blink. A guy who's three times her size. She moves like someone who's been waiting for this. Expecting insanity to come to her door. Not someone who just watches action movies, buys crap on the internet, and thinks that makes them Special Forces.

No, this woman is out here living it.

There's no TV Hannah can see, but there's a stack of books with multicolor Post-it notes stuck to the edges of pages marking the ideas Sloane must think are noteworthy. The titles along the book spines are hard to make out, but they all contain words like *psychopath*, *FBI*, *profilers*, and of course, *serial killer*. A non-fiction, true crime library on a subject she's already way too familiar with. A much shorter stack of books sits next to them. Worn-out paperback copies of all the Harry Potter books, *Pride and Prejudice*, and a few Agatha Christie novels. Perhaps Sloane's favorites to add some light to her otherwise pitch-black reading choices.

"None of this is necessary. I'm not a threat to any of you," the large man says, cocking his head toward his zip-tied hands. Winces again from his run-in with Sloane's fists, elbows, and feet. "Here to help you."

"Don't recall putting up a hand for help." Sloane slides her gun into her hip holster with a click, turns to Hannah. "You?"

Hannah shakes her head.

"Impressive." Nord is checking out the place

as well. Waves his hand around, making a big show of it. "You've been busy out here. Done a lot since you bounced from that place in Oregon. Or was it one of the Dakotas, then Oregon?"

Sloane doesn't bother responding. Hannah sees a map tacked to one of the wood walls. Red and green pins marking locations.

"So many places you've moved in and out of." Nord sighs. "I get them all jumbled up."

Hannah watches Sloane simmer.

"I'm sure it's hard for you to keep track too." Nord keeps at it. "But I am a little surprised you didn't go with something slightly more posh. More luxury living-like. Don't get me wrong, this is swell as hell, but considering the money you peeled off me..."

"Need to stretch it out. Make my money last." Sloane opens the lid to a cooler whose best days have long passed. Pulls out three beers with one grab. The melted ice drips from the bottle to the concrete floor. "You should try it."

Sloane hands a longneck to Hannah. She considers the large man, opens one, then motions to him. He fights the obvious desire in his eyes as he stares down the beer. Giving in, he shrugs out a *sure*. Sloane tilts the bottle, pouring some into his mouth. Reluctantly, she hands one to Nord.

153

Hates it, but he manages to mouth a thank you for the beverage.

"Besides." Sloane cracks one for herself. "Final girls aren't all that employable."

Hannah twists her beer open. The first sip is unbelievable. She closes her eyes, and for a second, she almost forgets all the crazy. Opens her eyes and takes a second gulp, sad to see the crazy is still around.

Pulling back the rag posing as a curtain, she gets a look behind the place. Outside is an old pickup truck, some patio furniture beyond their prime, and an easel with the beginnings of a new painting. A repurposed can of beans filled with paintbrushes sits on the ground.

"You do these?" Hannah thumbs toward the paintings hanging near the bed.

"I did."

They are a visceral smear of reds and blacks. Sprays of white mixed with undefinable colors pop off the canvas. Bold. Attention commanding. Some might say violent.

Hannah imagines Sloane throwing paint at the helpless canvas with all the rage she can summon. Looking deeper, getting closer to Sloane's work, something strikes her. The paintings all seem to have figures of people buried inside the smears of violence. Faceless shapes that fade back into deep rich colors that have overtaken them.

Hannah thinks of the story Nord told her.

About the corporate retreat in the woods. Stealing a quick glance, she sees a scar that runs down, curving across Sloane's sculpted tricep, wrapped up in the thorns of her tattoos. A snake of a wound. There's another scar where her neck and body meet. Oddly shaped. Like a tight series of healed puncture wounds with a smaller line under them. A forever mark of a killer's mouth on her.

Does she see it every time she looks in the mirror? Does she want to see it?

A constant reminder that will never let that day stray too far away from her mind. Hannah assumes there's all sorts of scars, inside and out, that this woman carries. Sloane locks eyes with her from across the room.

A silent, unnerving beat.

Sloane tosses her bottle into a trash can while her hard eyes drill into Hannah, as if searching inside of her. Makes Hannah want to run out into the desert and never look back.

"Okay." Sloane claps her hands. "Haven't

had this many people out here in... well, ever. Makes me tired. So, I'd love it if you'd all—"

"Look. Just have to put this out there—" Nord about to launch into a pitch of some sort.

"No." Sloane puts up a hand. Her face morphs into a middle finger. "I will not *look*. Cannot listen to your shit. You came to my home unannounced. Zero invitation given."

"To be fair, there's not a great way to get ahold of you."

The large man tries to cut in. "Excuse me."

Sloane moves in close to Nord.

Strikes Hannah that he doesn't seem to shrink this time. Not the scared little man he was before the big guy showed up. Sloane and Nord begin barking at one another, firing streams of words back and forth. Hard to make out what's even being said.

Hannah moves in. Keeps a safe distance but knows she can't let this boil into a full-on war. This woman might kill Nord, then try to stick Hannah in a hole out in the West Texas dirt. She looks to the large man. He's trying to tell them something.

"Wait." Hannah attempts to break up the verbal assault.

They keep at it. Faces red. Bodies coiled tight.

"Excuse me," the man tries again, louder.

"Stop!" Hannah screams.

Sloane and Nord pause, stepping back from one another, momentarily slipping out from their anger trance.

"Please." Hannah points to the large man. "He's trying to tell us something. Maybe we should hear him out."

Neither Sloane nor Nord admit defeat, but reluctantly turn their attention to him.

"Thank you." The large man looks to Nord.

Doesn't go unnoticed by Hannah, or Sloane.

"Why do you keep looking at him?" Sloane turns to Nord. "What the hell is going on?"

Nord feigns a lack of knowledge, and Hannah wants to strangle him for holding back whatever he's been keeping from her.

"Listen to me!" The man's voice booms so loud it shakes the metal walls. Face red. Eyes pleading. Clearing his throat, resetting, he moves off the wall with his back to the doorway. "You are not safe." His voice returns to a calm tone. An adult explaining something to unknowing children. "None of you are. Things have been put in motion that are very dangerous."

Fear spikes in Hannah. "What *things?*"

"I don't know everything. But I do know you need to be careful—"

A dull thunk ends his sentence.

His eyes pop wide as his mouth falls open choking for air.

His zip-tied hands make quick jerks trying to reach behind him, grasping at nothing as he drops down to his knees.

An axe is stuck deep in his back.

Behind him stands a man with a sack over his head. A potato sack or something like it. Slits cut with blue eyes burning through. Another slit cut for a mouth. He kicks the large man down to the floor.

Sloane becomes a statue. Feet stuck to the floor.

Hannah looks to her. She's gone. From force of nature to lifeless in a fraction of a second. Eyes distant. Empty. She's seen a ghost. Her gun holstered useless by her side. Lips can only whisper one word.

"No, no, no."

The man tugs the axe free. The sick slip of the blade from the man's flesh sends chills racing up Hannah's spine. Nord stumbles back, slamming into the metal wall so hard it rattles the room.

The man with the axe lurches toward them.

Hannah almost forgot she's holding a gun. She raises her arm, but her trembling hand tilts the barrel down, not used to the weight. Or the stark fear that feels like she's being pulled to the ground.

The man stops. Cocks his head like an animal assessing. Regrips the axe. Heavy breathing sucking in and out from behind the sack that shrouds his face.

A sudden calm comes over Hannah. No idea why, but she's found a place of peace inside the chaos. She grips her weapon with both hands, breathing in deep and pushing the air out slow and steady. Her pounding heart eases.

"Who are you?" she asks.

The man howls. Inhuman. Hannah can see his toothy smile, then a flash of his tongue through the slit cut in the sack. Her place of peace is rattled, yet she still holds the gun steady. The man draws the axe back, launching himself at her.

Hannah fires.

The bullet zips clear, punching a hole in the metal behind him.

Without pause he keeps raging her way. She squeezes the trigger again. The shot tears through his shoulder, spinning his massive body around. The axe clanks to the floor. Hannah sucks in a breath, keeping her gun on him.

The man whips around, landing a thundering punch to Hannah's jaw. The force of the blow is like nothing Hannah has ever experienced. She absorbs the crunch, the crack in her face. Spots form in her eyes. Somehow, she's on the floor without realizing she fell. Through the globs of white clouding her vision, she watches her gun slide across the floor.

She can feel the man standing above her.

He kicks at her ribs. A hard swat to the back of her head plants her flat on the floor. Through the growing fog, Hannah hears a scream.

"No!" Sloane pulls her gun.

The man swings at Sloane. She dodges the punch, pivots, comes back up with a kick to his gut followed by a knee under his chin. Stumbling back, the man manages to grab a chair, hurling it at Sloane, altering her aim. Before she can get a clean shot at him, the man is out the door. Sloane screams, unloading her gun at the space where the man was only a fraction of a second before.

The gunshots echo out into nothing.

From the floor, Hannah's sight flutters and fades, barely hanging on to the here and now. The world caves in on itself. Feels like she's slipping into a bathtub filled with warm milk.

She stops fighting. Allows it to overtake her.

Eyes flutter, then close.

SIXTEEN

Hannah is in the bathtub of her overpriced apartment.

Skin soaking in the warm water.

Weightless, only her flickering thoughts keeping her tethered to reality. The National playing. Wineglass under her fingertips.

She thinks of the envelope in the kitchen.

Remembers she hasn't opened it. Corny told her it contains a check. She should have taken that money and ran away while she had the chance. Of course, there was no way for her to possibly know what was coming. No way to imagine that in a few moments the police would be knocking at her door with the news of what Zach Winter had done.

What he did for her.

The floor under Hannah rumbles and shakes. She hears muted, muffled screams seeping in through the haze. As if she were lying in her soothing sanctuary as a dome protected her from the big bad world. Keeping her safe from what was happening a few feet, perhaps a few inches, from her. In her mind, she's smiling. Enjoying the freedom of not being part of this.

Deep down, she knows that's not the truth.

The beating she took from the crazed man with the axe put her down for this little break in life. She will be forced back in the mix soon enough.

Like it or not.

Fingers press down on her neck. Checking for a pulse, she imagines. Probably Sloane. A voice deep within Hannah's mind screams out to her. Must be Corny again. Her sister begs her to snap out of it.

Don't make that woman do this alone.

Hannah's eyes crack open.

Through the thick soup of her vision, she watches Sloane leap to the door as she ejects a magazine from her gun. She slams in a fresh one as the empty bounces off the floor a few inches from Hannah's face. Sloane trains her weapon back and forth, scanning the terrain as she races out the door after him.

Hannah shuts her eyes again.

Needs a few more moments. Please. Only a few more seconds of peaceful denial. A razor-sharp realization slashes across her psyche. She almost died today. Closer than she ever thought she'd be. *And for what?* Another thought cuts deep. She's been pulled into this nightmare without knowing the answer to the only question that matters.

Why me?

Thoughts, moments, memories collide into a synaptic car crash. She thinks of when she and Corny were little. Poor. Penniless. Fatherless. But they found a way to make each other laugh no matter how dark times or their mother got. Some moments more pitch-black than others.

Sometimes Mom would drink until she passed out.

Other times she would bring a man home.

They'd always leave the next morning, sometimes in the middle of the night. Getting what they wanted, then escaping before things got unnecessarily uncomfortable. Corny would take Hannah by the hand and lead her under their bed. From under their bed, they'd hear their mother's bed squeaking in the next room. The sounds of adults playing like adults. The walls were always paper-thin no matter where they moved to. Unfortunately.

The next day, Mom would throw away the bottles while telling herself and the girls that she was changing. That *that* would never happen again. To her credit, Mom's promise would last a month or more, but at some point, there would always be new bottles and new men in her bed.

Corny would hold Hannah's hand, offering the now familiar sisterly chant—*This is not your fault*. Hannah's mind shifts away, spinning memories toward something new.

Fast-forward a few years.

Corny and Hannah are a little older. Sort of adults. They are in one of the apartments they lived in together. Corny used to always sit on the couch, hold her hand and soothe Hannah when the world was too much to walk through. Hannah was always the one who felt things more.

Life hits you harder, Corny would say.

Hannah thinks of when Luna was born. A light to make life okay. She was at the hospital for the big day. The smiles. The joy. A show of love Hannah had only read about.

Her thoughts slam to Zach.

The way they used to talk so harmlessly at the coffee place. How, unbeknownst to her, each word she said, each look she casually gave, was creating a path leading to where she is now. Corny would say things like...

This is not your fault.

Thoughts crash. Memories bleed into one another. A swirl of color and sound leading her back to an unfortunately common scene. Corny holding her hand under their childhood bed. Hannah's heart racing. Eyes dancing. Corny trying to soothe, working to make it okay for her little sister.

From under the bed, Hannah and Corny would see feet moving toward them. *Is it one of those men? Is it Mama?* Corny squeezes Hannah's hand tight. They both hold their breath...

A hand grabs Hannah's shoulder. Shakes her hard.

Hannah's eyes pop open.

She looks up at Sloane. Her face is red, sweat dripping down her forehead.

"Feeling strong?" she asks.

Hannah nods a yes even though she knows

she's so far from anything that would resemble strong. Her face swells. Mouth dry. Body throbs.

Sloane holds her gun ready, checks behind her, disbelief in her eyes that the man with the axe is gone. She offers a hand to Hannah, pulling her up to her feet. Hannah's sight is still sketchy but improving. Ears hold a dull ring. Hard to tell if it's the gunfire or the blows she took from a madman that has turned her mind to mush. Can't help but feel a little cool that she went toe to toe with a psycho killer.

"You okay?" Sloane asks.

"Not at all."

"You'll get used to that."

"Hey." Nord is still pressed against the wall, legs shaking, palms planted flat against the metal as if searching for a handle to the world. "What... what the hell was that?"

Hannah and Sloane look to one another for answers that neither one has.

As the adrenaline slips, acknowledgment of what just happened grabs Hannah by the throat. Her illusions of control flutter and fade. A madman tried to kill them. Not something that happens in everyday life. Until recently, death was a far-off, distant concept. Something that should happen at a hospital several decades from now.

Today, death is all too real.

Her breathing becomes labored. The cool and calm she had earlier has turned to dust.

"He was going to kill us," slips from her mouth.

"No shit." Sloane bursts into motion. As if a switch was flipped, she rushes to the back of the house. "That's the kind of laser-sharp analysis you're going to need."

Hannah looks to Nord. She finds some comfort in the fact he's responding far worse than she is. He now sits on the floor, knees pulled up near his chest, staring out the door. She can see his thoughts rumbling behind his blank expression. Impossible to read.

Hannah's eyes slip over the large man's body on the floor, the seeping gash fresh and slick. Blood pooling around him. Her world tilts.

She pulls her phone. Needs to speak to someone who'll stabilize her. A conversation with Corny is required. Some violence-induced vision of them under their childhood bed isn't going to cut it. Not today.

"What the hell are you doing?" Sloane storms back into the room. She has a packed go-bag over one shoulder and another, longer unzipped bag over the other. She also holds a large can by the handle, its contents sloshing against the can's metal walls. "Drop that phone."

"I'm calling my sister."

"No."

"Wasn't asking."

"Did I miss where you actually have a clue what's going on here?"

"I don't care." Hannah's finger hovers above the glass of the phone. "This is happening."

"Look. I get it." Sloane drops the go-bag at her feet and splashes the contents of the can around the room. The kitchen first. "You watched someone get killed with an axe. It's a shocking thing, no argument here, but unfortunately, it's not my first."

The thick smell of gas fills the air.

"That guy with the sack on his head? He found this place. Not sure how, but that's not a good thing." Sloane pours gas over the counter. Splashing, dripping down to the floor. "If you didn't notice, I've worked hard to make this place unfindable. So..." She drops the empty can with a hollow clank, then starts shoving guns into the empty bag. "My best guess is that freak with the axe followed the dead guy on the floor, who was apparently following you two to my home."

"Sloane..." Nord coughs. "We need to discuss what in the hell—"

"No." Sloane shoves her gun under his chin. "I saw the way that dead guy looked at you. He knew you." Nord looks away. Sloane presses the gun harder, pushing his head up to meet her stare. "Should we start the discussion there?"

Hannah's mind hits rewind.

There was a moment before the axe. It wasn't much, but Hannah does remember seeing some sort of connection between Nord and the dead man.

"What's your plan?" Hannah asks Sloane as her hand moves nice and easy toward the gun she dropped while fighting the madman. "I mean, it looks like we all have pieces of information that might—I don't know—might help keep us alive."

She pockets her phone. Have to call Corny later.

"Doing fine alone. I'm not looking for puzzle buddies." Sloane's eyes drill into Nord. "I could kill you. You get that, right? Bullet in your head, plant the gun in the hand of the dead guy on the floor. Set this whole thing on fire and let the cops figure it out." She shifts the gun between his eyes, taking a step back. Nord swallows hard. "Might not be so bad. Think about it. You'd be the great, brave investigative whatever-the-hell who died getting his big story." Sloane gives a dead stare. "What do you think?"

"Sloane, you don't want that." Nord's voice cracks as he points at Hannah. "She's right. There's all kind of things you don't know. We can help each other."

"Yeah. Let me think about it..." Sloane nods, presses her lips together. "Hell no."

"Think," Hannah says.

Sloane turns. Hannah has a gun on her.

"This is stupid. We need each other. You're probably not wrong; there's a very good chance bad people know where we are. So, if that's true, then the math on this is simple."

"Is it now?" Sloane lowers her gun from Nord's face.

"I think so." Hannah lowers her gun in a sign of trust. Looks toward the pooling gasoline in the kitchen area. "Let's light this candle, then find a better spot to chat this shit through."

SEVENTEEN

ZACH SITS at the back of a church.

The massive sanctuary's square footage rivals an average Walmart.

Row after row of polished, gleaming wood pews that curve into circular seating face what could best be described as something half stage, half altar. Zach's high school football stadium was smaller than this.

He'd driven here under the cover of early morning darkness and watched the sun rise as he passed through the city limits of tiny Texas town after tiny Texas town. Left the truck he stole from the motel last night in the parking lot of a roadside diner, then grabbed a quick breakfast before finding a new ride in the parking lot of a trashy bar a few blocks over. Probably left there overnight by someone currently sleeping off a big night in the small town.

Lifting up the lid, the screen shifts from black to gray to corporate logo as he fires up a fresh laptop. Zach checks the VPN, then connects to the church's Wi-Fi. The hard drive hums along the tops of his thighs. He'd cracked the laptop he used last night over his knee, snapping it like a twig, then microwaved the hard drive at a convenience store while the clerk was in the back.

The organ plays a tune Zach vaguely remembers from when he was a kid.

His mother had dragged him, his brother, and sister to church every Sunday. Not sure if today is Sunday or some other day of religious significance. A weary brain thinking like a weary man. Zach shakes his head hard, busting loose the cobwebs. Angry at himself for not reading the area. Using what the terrain is telling him.

Find some focus.

Stop. Read what's in front of you.

Considering the sanctuary is only half full, it must be an off day. This is no Sunday crowd. He didn't hate going to church when he was young, but he always felt like he didn't get it. Felt it was a room full of adults pretending to be decent. Faking kindness once a week in order to get some kind of cosmic credit. Punch a ticket to the promised land.

Thoughts pop, focus slips, bending into a mess of nothing and everything. His mind comes to a screaming halt, freezing on a single mental image.

Fresh blood. Sprayed against a wall.

Thick blobs, then spreading, thinning out into droplets across a motel room. The room that was next door to his. All that deep crimson raised up plump along the wall mere seconds before he stole the drunken lovebird's truck.

Heart racing, shutting his eyes tight, Zach shakes it off.

He'd killed the man before he had a chance to say a word, let alone put up a fight. The woman's scream was so loud... then so quiet. Surprising how dull the feeling was to him. Not the sharp stick of emotion he'd had at Gareth's house. There was no buzz. No hum at the back of his skull after he killed the lovebirds at the motel. More like he'd checked a box. A task successfully completed.

He was glad the truck keys were on the nightstand and easy to find. Didn't want to waste what was left of the dark searching. Needed to get clear of the Austin area as fast as possible. Get the hell gone.

The laptop screen lights up.

Zach's eyes dart around the church, scanning to see if people are looking at him. If any of the congregation is checking out the stranger sitting among them. Their attention is firmly on the Lord and the song in the air, as it should be.

He'd told the elderly man at the front door he was there to work on the church's network. Showed him his laptop. The old man said something about someone named Carol and all that funky computer stuff. Zach smiled, gave a shrug, and the old man laughed and patted him on the back, welcomed him in.

Pulling up a browser window, Zach goes immediately to the site.

Body vibrates with excitement. The anticipation is killing him. Dying to know what's being said. His fingers fast-tap out the username and password, then he hits Log In.

He can't hide his smile.

The board is flooded with posts.

Posts filled with words talking about Zach. About what he's done. There are even a few memes. Crude and tasteless, but they are all about him. They've put Hannah's face on some brightly colored anime torture sex porn. Pictures of the house. Video swipes of Zach covered in red and blue lights holding a gun to that woman's head. The words used in the posts are profane but encouraging, in their own way.

He fucking did it!!!

Hunt that bitch down!!!

For her... for us, brutha!!!

His fingertips touch the screen. Wants to feel the words. Wants them to become part of him. Warmth fills his chest. Blinking away tears, he scrolls and reads over the well-wishers. Pride swells as all the acknowledgement, the validation, washes over him. For the first time in as long as he can remember, he feels seen. Heard.

Then one user catches his eyes.

A user more vocal than the others. One whose words have a little more spice to them than the others. Zach squints as he reads.

This user says Zach is weak.

That he's clumsy.

Lazy. Sloppy.

Goes as far as to say he is going to take matters into his own hands. Show everyone *how to get shit done.*

Zach digs into the handle. *Better_thanyour_-Better.* It's been around for a while but hasn't been very active. Not until recently. Not until Zach did what he'd done.

Zach's eyes move up and down the screen.

Not sure when he started holding his breath.

Tapping and scrolling along the mousepad, he tries not to let the *Better_thanyour_Better* get to him. Forces the user's words out from his head. Most people on here are posing, projecting what they want to be. Never escalating past the screen. *Mental masturbation artists* he saw someone call them. But there are some who do more than watch. Some *transcend the glass,* as they say. Put some skin and bone on the digital world.

Zach can't be bothered with those who aren't ready to jump into analog reality. Pull themselves out from the sea of false bravado on the site. He moves on, feverously searching for a post from one person on the site in particular. The only one who truly matters. His words mean everything to the people on here. Zach is absolutely no exception.

Scrolling farther and farther down, his heart pounds. It's not there. Nothing.

That can't be possible.

He has to have seen what Zach has done.

Zach's stomach twists. He picks the laptop up and slams it down on his knees. An older woman singing alone in a pew across from him fires him a look. Zach ignores her empty threat. He balls his fists tight, shakes his hands loose, then starts scanning the screen from the top again, moving line by line.

Maybe he somehow missed the comment. The Administrator's words. His acknowledgement of what Zach has done. So much chatter on the board about the house and what Zach did. Too much for the Administrator to miss.

Not possible. Had to have noticed.

Then Zach sees the post. Not from the Administrator. No cryptic message about connecting the dots or what's between the words that saves or slaughters. Zach holds his breath. There is a video.

A video posted by *Better_thanyour_Better*.

The time stamp is from this morning. There are streams of comments under the video. So much more there than for Zach's deeds. Most praising the user with strong cheers and venom. Calling Zach a joke, a clown, a little bitch, and endless varieties of homophobic slurs. Calling him out for not finishing the job. One says Zach is *pissing his panties over taking it to the next level.*

The title of the post is **better_than_zach_winter**.

Zach's shaking finger taps a click. The video starts.

There's a man wearing a sack covering his head. Slits cut out for the eyes. Another for his mouth. A toothy smile under the sack. The sun blazes overhead. The man wearing the sack doesn't say a word. The wind mixed with his heavy breathing is the only soundtrack.

The camera turns around.

The video jerks left and right, blurring the images, before it levels out. The camera seems to snap into place, maybe a chest cam or some sort. It's a wide-open desert. There's a makeshift home up ahead with a deck. Looks like it's been pieced together with some kind of metal storage containers.

The man moves an axe into view.

Moving in quick and quiet, making a sweeping circle, staying out of view, the camera POV comes up behind a large man standing in the doorway. The axe pulls back out of frame, then plants into the man's back. The dying man falls away from the screen.

Zach sees Hannah Rush staring back at the screen. Eyes wide. Full of fear. Next to her is someone who looks so familiar. Zach holds his breath. *It can't be.*

Is that the final girl? The one they always talk about on the board?

Public Enemy #1, they call her.

The Prize Kill, Prettier Dead, others say. The one nobody could find.

The image freezes. A still frame of everything this site is about. The big prize of the girl who got away from Logan Burke is standing next to Hannah, the new *it girl* of the site. Both with frightened looks staring back for everyone to see.

Zach's eyes drift below the video.

There's a comment from a user with the handle Dotts_The_Administrator. Dotts runs the board. Runs the hearts and minds of everyone on the site. Zach's eyes fill. The two-word comment from the Administrator sends him crashing down.

Fantastic work.

Zach tries to push everything down. Shoves it all down deep inside himself and locks it away kicking and screaming. Refuses his internal request to process the punishment of his own emotions.

Get your focus back, man.

He has a plan. It's working, just takes time.

He can't get pulled into this bullshit. He tries to find his discipline, but it drifts away like burning paper in the wind.

A valiant effort until that final comment. *Fantastic work.*

Those two words burn a hole through his very soul.

Must return to before. Hit pause, rewind and find the time he was zeroed in on his plan. The other user is a flash in the pan. Not the truth. Not like Zach.

Quietly, he recites Dotts_The_Administrator's mantra.

Connect the dots, man. It's what's between the words.

It's the in-betweens that can save us. Or slaughter us.

EIGHTEEN

Bobby Greene bites down on a stick.

The bullet he took to the shoulder burns like absolute hell.

He's fairly sure it went straight through but damn it hurts something awful. Still has some movement. Limited mobility but it still has utility. Knows he has to keep it clean until he can get actual medical treatment. Despite the pain, he can't help but feel good about what he's done today.

The Administrator called it *fantastic work.*

Bobby is in the mix now.

The life he's wanted is no longer theoretical. This is the real world. The fleshy analog that favors the bold.

He sits on the lowered toilet seat in a truck

stop bathroom just off the highway with a convenience store attached. It was just busy enough for Bobby to get through unnoticed with his backpack. Used his jacket to cover up his wound well enough to get past the cashier and the handful of patrons. But this next part is going to be pretty miserable.

He can't believe that bitch got a shot off.

More pissed that he let it happen.

He expected the final girl to be a problem, but not that Austin twat Zach Winter had zeroed in on. *Zach Winter.* Little bitch can't do anything. A big nothing. Talk, talk, talk. Tap, tap, tapping at the keyboard. All from little bitch boy Zach.

Bobby doesn't know what Zach's handle is on the site—people change them all the time, some don't even use one—but he can narrow it down to a select few little poser freaks. Bobby has analyzed the posts. Easy for him to tell who might be for real and who is a big nothing. Dopey fucks typing bullshit all day just for show.

Hasn't checked the site since he sat down—been a little busy—but he's guessing bitch boy Zach is beyond pissed about the video he posted.

Smiles huge.

Truly better than Zach Winter.

Using his phone's camera, reversing the POV, he gets a better angle on the shoulder wound then tap-snaps a picture. Turning the phone around, he spreads the image wide to get a good look at what he's dealing with here.

Yeah, it looks to be a through and through. He got some field training before he was discharged from the military after there were some reported issues about him. Violent behavior. Lack of emotional control. Same words and phrases that keep popping up from job to job. Town to town. Woman to woman.

What's a sweet, simple boy from Shreveport supposed to do?

He decided to stop talking to everyone after he lost his late-night shift at the convenience store. Teenage girls got chatty with the cops about some things he said to them. They said Bobby tried to touch one of them. Like really touch one of them. He moved from place to place. A night on his mom's couch before she threw him out. Slept in his car for few nights. The park. All around Shreveport.

He needed a job, but more importantly, he needed an angle.

He pretended he was deaf for a while, thinking the sympathy vote might open some doors, but didn't know how to sign. Tried to get a quick study via some YouTube videos but didn't do it enough to be convincing. Made up a story that an accident took his hearing recently.

That didn't work either.

Potential employers didn't buy his story no matter how good Bobby thought it was. His baby face and (false) laidback demeanor had gotten him through much of life, but deep down he knew he might have reached the limit of that would get him.

He started spending his days drinking all the cheap wine he'd stolen from the store—still thinks it's funny he didn't get fired for that—and really started to dig in to what he was meant to do with his life.

All night deep searches, scratching the insides of his own mind. He'd let the wine peel back the layers and simply let his brain flow in any and every direction it wanted. Then, late one night teetering on morning, he stumbled across something.

He found this site. Not easy to find—he lucked out and wormed an invite out of someone by trading a few gigs of his best underage porn for a login—but so worth it.

It unlocked a community of good folk.

People who shared some of his points of view. They posted endless streams of words and memes and things that made a lot of sense to him. He devoted hours to the site. Skipped eating and sleeping to study it. Knew this was where he had found his tribe.

The more he read, the more he realized there were so many people who were looking for a leader, but no one had the balls to point the way.

No one except the Administrator, of course.

Hope he's who they say he is.

What Zach did was cute, might even have impressed some people, but it was nothing compared to what Bobby was prepared to do. Once he saw the news light up his feed about what went down in Austin, Bobby drove as fast as he could from Louisiana to get there. To find this Hannah Rush who meant so much to Zach.

This was the universe giving him an in. A doorway to greatness.

Hell, that nice lady on the news showed him right where her apartment was and everything. Bobby parked outside her building waiting, thinking of a plan, then he saw this 4Runner leave the garage. He wasn't sure, but it seemed odd for someone to leave the building at that hour of the morning so he followed. Then, to his delight, he watched the SUV park a few miles away. His stomach tingled as he watched Hannah Rush slide out the back and into the passenger seat.

Bobby grunts, bites down on the stick a little harder.

From his backpack, he pulls a Ziploc filled with gauze pads. He'd put together a bag with some items he thought might come in handy. Tried to think of best—and worst—case scenarios. The zip-ties could be considered *best*. The gauze pads and other assorted medical items would fall under *worst*. He knows he needs to stop the bleeding from his shoulder. Needs to buy himself time to finish this thing with Hannah and the final girl.

He's so close he can taste it. Can taste them.

Just like Logan Burke.

Sweat drips from his forehead as he pulls pads from the bag. Wiping the drops from his skin, he sucks his fingertips dry thinking of Hannah. He'd followed them into West Texas. Watched her and that little man go to a motel. Monitored every step as she went into her room, and he went into his. He thought about moving on Hannah there, bursting into the room and taking care of what Zach couldn't do right then and there.

But it didn't seem right. Something was off. Something at the back of his mind told him to wait for a better moment. A better show.

And man, oh man was he right.

He didn't realize it at the time, how could he, but Hannah was about to lead him to the biggest prize of them all—the final girl.

He checks his phone.

The tracking device he has on the final girl's truck shows they are still in Texas. Not too far from where he is but not close enough. He needs to get himself right and get back on the road. Must stay somewhat close to them or the tracking will get wonky as hell or go bye-bye completely.

He's using one of those hi-tech luggage tags on that old truck of hers. Stuck it just inside the metal lid that grants access to the gas cap and secured it with some gum. The tags are very effective, but the range isn't crazy huge and can get more unreliable the farther out you get.

Bobby pockets his phone. Time to stop dicking around with this.

Deep breath. Teeth dig into the stick.

He stuffs the gauze deep into his wound with his fingers. Like stuffing a turkey.

The pain is like nothing he's ever felt before. He pushes farther and farther, hoping he doesn't pass out. This is so much worse than getting shot in the first place. There's a moment where he thinks he might snap the stick in half with his teeth. Worried he might choke on the wood.

He tries to focus on anything other than the blazing fire in his shoulder. Consciousness fades, then slams back.

He sits up straight on the toilet. Whips his head back and forth, spits the stick out, then slams the back of head against the tile. His heart rate had to break two hundred.

Slams his head again.

His vision blurs, but he feels the rat-tat drumbeat heart coming down now. Far from normal, but decreasing at least. Sucks deep breaths in and out. In and out.

Pulling his phone back out from his pocket, he checks the site.

Rereading comments from the Administrator makes the pain all but disappear. He thinks of the bottle of codeine he lifted off his mother. He'll grab a Dr. Pepper on the way out and toss back a few of Mama's little pills. He smiles big. A chuckle rolls from his belly up to his throat, catching it before it can escape his body. Stopping the laughter from reaching the world.

Bobby places a shaky finger to his lips, shushing himself like a child.

Like his mama used to do to him when she'd shut his bedroom door to spend time with a brand new man-friend.

He silently mouths the words...

My better is better than your better, Zach.

NINETEEN

"You DIDN'T NEED to torch my ride." Nord shifts in his chair. Its semi-wood construction could crumble to the diseased carpet any moment. "Really didn't. All I'm saying."

"Shut the hell up," Sloane whisper-barks back.

Lying on the bed, Sloane stares up at the multiple dark spots that pepper the ceiling.

Hannah sits perched on a beaten-up dresser across the room from them. Seemed like the safest place to be. Tries hard not to be grossed out thinking about what that bed has been through. Craning her neck, she looks up to get a look at the same spots Sloane is staring at. Reminds her of a decaying map of Asia.

They'd found a cheap roadside motel off

Highway 87, miles away from what's left of Sloane's home.

Sloane made a strong case they should take her truck, considering she paid cash for it off a kid who didn't ask questions. Dude didn't even have her name. Seemed safer than a fancy SUV registered in the name of a journalist who's already been confirmed to have been followed. Nord agreed, not knowing that he was agreeing to Sloane setting his 4Runner on fire.

Oddly enough, she didn't torch the big man's sedan.

Slashed the tires and checked it for anything useful but didn't set it on fire. Hannah couldn't help but feel bad watching Sloane ransack the man's car. Didn't seem right to dig through the belongings of someone who died moments ago. Wallet. Phone. Glove box. Seemed cold. Logically it made sense, he wasn't using anything in that car anymore, but still. She'd refused to help Sloane and Nord drag the man's body into the back of the car. Sloane said it was to create confusion about the scene.

Hannah can't place the feeling she had while watching it all unfold, but it still clings to her like a film covering her skin. If that man had come there to protect her, he deserved better than what happened to him.

She imagines what's still burning back there.

Flames from Sloane's safe house licking the big blue West Texas sky. Fire moving in a heat-on-heat dance in middle of the plains. Hannah agrees with Nord on one thing. Setting Nord's car on fire was a little unnecessary. Making Nord squirm was good fun if she's being honest, but unnecessary. Lighting up Sloane's makeshift home tracked, however. Perhaps it deleted any trace of them being there. Hopefully it worked.

Sloane said it all leaves something for law enforcement to dig into.

An extra pit to travel down into rather than simply a missing journalist. What was left back there creates questions. Opens mystery boxes in the minds of cops. Same reason they put that man in the back of his own car. A dead body with an axe wound. A missing journalist's 4Runner burning from a gasoline fire, along with a house made of repurposed shipping containers that doesn't have an owner of record.

Why is this SUV on fire? Who lived out here? What happened to the large man in the car?

Did they all know each other? Drugs? Human trafficking?

All the above?

Sloane said the more questions you can create, the more time it takes for them to understand which questions are important. Buys time, and time is expensive as hell in this life.

"This place truly sucks." Nord lifts himself up from the chair, then drops back down. "Think I liked your little desert death house better than—"

"You two wanted to chat it up," Hannah cuts him off, saving them from whatever crap Nord was about to share. Looks straight to Sloane. "What now, final girl?"

"Hmmm." Sloane keeps staring at the ceiling. "Fresh out of big ideas."

Hannah can tell she's working on some new big ideas, if she was ever out of them to begin with. Seems unlikely. The wheels constantly turn like mad in that mind of hers.

"Well, you were obviously ready if trouble came your way." Hannah pushes off the dresser and starts pacing. Moving helps her process. "You had everything ready to go. Gas cans and go-bag packed. Able to slip back into ghost mode in a snap."

"Had it ready. Really didn't want to use it." Sloane cracks her knuckles in front of her face, then slips her hands behind her head again. "What I'd really love to know is how your buddy Nord over there knew that big guy who took an axe to the spine."

"What?" Nord fires up straight.

Hannah stops pacing. She can see it all over his face. He's hiding something beyond big.

"You know." Sloane turns her head to him. "The large gentleman who died in front of us. He knew you. Pretty sure you knew him."

"Well, I did not know him. Truly don't understand whatever you're grinding on—"

"She's right." Hannah remembers the moment Sloane's grilling Nord on. There was recognition between them. That moment got shoved down by the events of the day, under-standable, but she can see clear as day now. "You two knew each other."

The room goes silent. Pin-drop silent as Sloane and Hannah wait for Nord to say some-thing. Anything. The gears of his mind grind, then he finally speaks.

"It's not like that."

"Okay, Nord." Sloane makes a quick spin on her back, sits up, plants her feet on the floor with a thump. "What's it like, then?"

On instinct, Hannah steps toward the door,

not realizing that she moved there to block him from running. *Is this who I am now?* Always looking for angles. Exits and entry points.

The air in the room pulls tight. Nord squirms. His usual quick wit and so-so charm have all but vanished, leaving him when he needs his tools the most.

Sloane raps her fingers on her knee, waiting. Expressionless but her message is clear.

Hannah can see what's next. Sloane will escalate quick to the violence phase. Start aggressively hurting him if Nord doesn't give them something. And soon.

Hannah's eyes plead with him. *Say it.*

"I didn't lie to you..." Nord clears his throat. "I don't know him. But I believe him. Someone sent him."

Sloane's eyes bounce to Hannah. Hannah wants to push off the door, launch, then strangle Nord herself.

"My brother-in-law's firm didn't send him, did they?" she asks.

"Doubtful."

"Who did?" Sloane's words flat and cold.

"Can't tell you what I don't know."

"Bullshit."

"Believe what you want—"

"What the hell do you know?" Hannah feels a click in her head. Breathes in deep, begging for calm to creep in. "Happen to know the guy with the axe? Did you know he was coming?"

"No." He stands. "Of course not. Are you kidding me?"

"Zach?" Hannah is in his face now. Calm isn't coming her way. "Did you know what Zach was doing?"

"No. No. No. That's not it." Eyes bulging, he looks for understanding as he slumps back down into the chair. "I didn't know anything about what happened at that house with Zach. No idea that he was killing people because he was crushing hard."

"Then what?" Sloane stands over him next to Hannah. "Spill it."

Seconds pound like a hammer. Nord fidgets. Sweat forms. Sloane pulls a tactical blade from her ankle, moves toward Nord's throat. Hannah tries to grab her shoulder. Sloane slaps it back.

"Sloane..." Hannah is careful not to touch her. Like dealing with a live wire. "We need to know what he knows."

"Not sure we do."

"He's all we've got. Look around." Hannah spreads her arms out wide. "We're in a shit motel room after fleeing a burning crime scene. After a guy with an axe tried to cut us to chunks. Not to mention, the guy with the axe looked a lot like the last guy who tried to hack you up."

Sloane is in a slow burn, but Hannah can tell her words are worming their way into her mind. She doesn't want to hear any of it, but Hannah is beginning to make sense.

Sloane exhales, pauses, then puts the blade away. For now.

"This guy, this clown, is the only source of information we have." Hannah moves nice and slow, closer to Nord. "You really need to tell us something. Something super special."

Nord sucks in a deep breath. His eyes dance inside his skull. Mind searching for what to say. How to say it. Putting up a hand, he asks for a moment. Hannah looks to Sloane, hoping cooler heads have arrived.

Sloane takes a step back, sitting down on the side of the bed.

"There's this site. A sort of web forum. A chan board. Image board, they're sometimes called. Most of these boards are harmless. Sometimes even informative or fun. But this one?" Nord swallows. "It's hard to find, brings in people by invitation only. The term dark web gets overused, but that's where it lives. The site's had to jump from various service providers from time to time. Oregon, then to Russia. Was out of Brazil for a beat, then back to Washington state. I heard they might have found a small haven of sorts in Oklahoma. Tiny town, I think. Need to spend more time on—"

Hannah snaps her fingers an inch from his nose to stop the drift in his babbling.

Nord resets, starts up again.

"In order to survive, the site had to bounce around is what I'm saying. Most platform protection services won't touch it. There's a few that say freedom of speech has to be protected at all costs, no matter the speech. So, a very few of these outlier providers allow this site to exist until the heat from regulators is too much to handle or the feds lean hard on them—"

"Okay," Hannah interrupts. "Got it. But what the hell does any of this have to do with anything?"

"Some people believe, like the people on this site, the one I'm talking about that floats from shadow to shadow..." Nord's voice trails off as he looks around. "Can I get some water?"

Sloane cracks her knuckles. "No."

"What do they believe, Nord?"

He breathes in deep, exhales, then stares down as he speaks.

"Some of the users have a handle. Not a requirement, but some like to name themselves for show. A bullshit name—some funny, some not —they use on the site to comment, post memes, links, videos, or whatever. Helps everyone hide to a certain degree, but there's one person who runs the board. The Administrator. This person can help push the conversation in a direction. Moderates in a targeted way. But in this case, on this board, the administrator is treated more like... well, like a god."

Hannah and Sloane share a look.

"You understand what I'm trying to say here?" Nord looks up. "They really see him as a god. This Administrator, he's got some catch-phrases he throws around. Connecting the dots and all kinds of creepy shit."

Hannah can see the words *connecting the dots* hit Sloane hard. Her spine went straight as a board the second he said it. Hannah had also seen something like that when she was researching Sloane on the internet. A phrase about *connecting the dots* was used during the corporate retreat massacre. The killer said it over and over again.

"Nord. Again," Hannah says. "What does all that have to do with us?"

"The guy who runs this site, this Administrator? Their god?" Nord locks eyes with Sloane. "It's believed he's someone you know."

Sloane's face wipes clean, leaving zero expression.

"Who?" Hannah's heart falls. "Who is it?"

"They believe that he's..." Nord swallows hard. "Logan Burke."

TWENTY

Logan Burke.

The killer who butchered Sloane's friends and coworkers that night.

A benign corporate retreat that became a moonlight bloodbath. And now, someone has decided to pose as him on a deep, dark website that celebrates what he's done. To make it worse, someone made the decision to dress up as a looka-like of that insane killer and attack Sloane's safe house in the middle of nowhere.

Tracked her down.

Found her. A human needle in a global haystack.

Are there multiple Logan Burke wannabes out there roaming the world?

Is that even possible?

Or worse, could Logan Burke still be alive?

Hannah fights to process it all, sifting through the remains of logic after Nord dropped that bomb on them moments ago. She thinks of the fake Logan Burke she fought. The one who did kill someone in cold blood, shaking the three people in this cheap motel room.

He murdered the large man who said he was sent there to protect them.

And Nord had some connection with the man who was killed.

All the twists and turns spin like a mental tornado, only to break apart, sending shards cutting, slicing Hannah's sanity into bits.

How is all this even possible? Who would want to follow that?

Who would delude themselves into believing that crazed killer was alive, let alone someone they should follow?

None of it lands.

Oddly shaped pieces to a puzzle that began when Zach murdered three people in her name. But the number of pieces multiplies by the hour.

"That's insane. Logan died." Sloane stands up. "I know this because I killed him."

Nord seems to curl into himself while sitting in the chair, like a dog anticipating a beating.

"Sloane." Hannah hops off the dresser. "Let's hear him out."

Sloane's jaw tightens. Fists clench.

Hannah keeps her tone as even as she can. "That guy back at your place. Is there any chance it was him? Could it have been Logan Burke?"

Sloane stops. Blank, arrested expression. Her hard stare slips over toward Hannah. Eyes fill as her hesitation stretches—the push and pull to answer her question.

"Zero," she finally says. "No chance that it was him."

Sloane's swelling emotion, plus the pause before her answer, hits Hannah like a runaway train.

She isn't sure.

Sloane wants so badly to be sure—and maybe there's only the thinnest shred of doubt—but there's enough doubt there to shake her to the bone.

Hannah works it through.

How could a man rampage through a camp of people, survive what Sloane did to him, then escape from wherever the cops took him?

There had to be a hospital. A morgue.

Then, even if he did escape, there's no way in today's world with eyes everywhere that an escaped mass murderer could run around free without being noticed. That's a true crime, click-bait story if ever there was one.

Hannah looks to Sloane. Even with all that logic stacking, there's a thin sliver of doubt. Just enough to reduce this powerful, resilient, battle-tested woman down to rubble.

Hannah resets. "Okay. And that wasn't Zach Winter either. Sack Face was too big. Zach isn't that tall. So..." Hannah levels her stare on Nord. "Who the hell was he?"

"I don't know. How would I—"

"But you're thinking he has something to do with this site, right? This bullshit thing that worships Logan Burke?"

"That would make sense. Sure."

Sloane puts a foot in the middle of Nord's chest. The chair flings back, pinning him against the wall. Sloane pushes hard. Nord can't speak, only cough and gasp. She pulls back. His chair slams back to the floor. Before he can take a breath, Sloane has her tactical blade out and an inch from his eyeball.

He looks to Hannah for protection.

She shrugs. *Sorry, bro.*

Hannah peeks over Sloane's shoulder at him. "I've tried to help you. This is the part where you need to help yourself. You've been working on a book, correct? You know a ton about this woman here, right? The one with the knife at your eyeball?"

Nord nods.

"You have a deep understanding of what she's capable of?"

Another nod. Sweat drips.

"Cool, cool. So, while you've been working on that book, all that research, it sounds like you've done a deep dive into this site. The inner workings. That safe to say?"

"Yes."

Sloane stands like a statue, elbow locked with her blade ready to strike. Burning with a special kind of hate. Hannah thinks of the detectives who grilled her at her apartment. The cliché good cop/bad cop. She's a quick study on their tactics.

"So, it's also safe to say you could give us all kinds of information about this site. Perhaps even help us—oh, I don't know—find this Administrator guy."

"I don't know who he is. No clue where he is either."

The knife moves even closer, the tip a minimal push away from piercing the pupil.

"I don't! I'm telling the truth! But I'll give you everything I have. I will." A trembling mess. "We can work something out. There's money to be made here."

Hannah closes her eyes. Can't believe that's his answer.

Sloane flinches. "Yeah, I'm taking his eye."

"No! Wait! Please. Let's go somewhere else. I can take you somewhere that might have some answers. We should be moving anyway. You don't want to be stationary too long, believe me."

Sloane looks to Hannah.

"There's so much I can tell you. We can work together. We can all get what we want out of this."

"All I want is to not be chased by crazy people." Hannah looks to Sloane.

"Yeah." Sloane lowers the knife. "Same."

"Perfectly reasonable." Nord holds his heart. Checks his pulse. "I can help."

Sloane ignore him. Looks to Hannah. Too long for Hannah's tastes.

"What?"

"I'm not above doing what has to be done to end this." Sloane's stare bores a hole in Hannah. "You? You really prepared to kill someone?"

Hannah doesn't answer. Unsure of the full weight of the question.

"You were pretty quick to redline back at my place. Went hard against that Logan Burke fanboy."

"You really sure it wasn't Logan?" Hannah asks.

"If this gets super ugly, and it will," she says, ignoring Hannah's question, "do you have it in you?"

Hannah's mind drifts. The idea of killing someone. Something she hadn't really considered. Never had to.

"I can't trust Nord. He's a five-star weasel." Sloane springs into action, not waiting for Hannah's thoughts to solidify. Starts wiping down the doorknob, then strips the bed's sheets and pillowcases. "Love to have someone on my side—could be a refreshing change of pace—but not a necessity."

Hannah promises nothing but doesn't say no either. Would like to hang on to her final answer if she can.

Thinks of Corny. Thinks of Luna.

Sloane reaches in her bag and tosses a pack of wipes to her. Hannah catches it in midair, snapping her out of her trance.

"While you're thinking shit over, wipe down everything we might have touched." Sloane balls up the sheets from the bed. "Nord's right about one thing. We need to keep moving. These assholes have proven proficient in finding us. Also need to make like we were never here."

"Where are we going?" Hannah pulls out a wipe, working over the bathroom doorknob.

"Nord seems to have a lead in Oklahoma, right?" Sloane shoves the sheets into Nord's chest. "Luckily, that's not all that far from here."

"More of a theory than what I'd call a rock-solid lead."

"You got any stronger theories?"

Nord shakes his head no.

"Then Oklahoma it is." Sloane places her hands on his shoulders. Squeezes tight. "Just so we're clear, you continue hiding things? I'm going to remove body parts. One by one until your last words request the sweet release of death."

"Sloane..." Nord tries to talk his way out. "Please, this doesn't have to—"

Sloane pinches his lips closed with her fingers.

Hannah watches. Half-enjoying it. Half terrified. Knows her threat is not theoretical. It could easily become the true story about the demise of Nord.

She wants to talk to her sister.

Wants to be under their childhood bed holding her hand, listening to her big sister tell her soothing things. There's no way to explain everything to Corny, but if Hannah doesn't find some stable ground soon, she's going to spin out into a place she might not ever come back from. Needs to keep her head together now more than ever.

Corny has been tasked with that job her entire life.

"Once we get out of here, I'm calling my sister." Hannah pulls her gun from behind her back, letting it hang by her side. "Again, to be clear, not asking."

Sloane smiles. Eyes flare as if she likes what she sees.

A chill rips through Hannah. *Am I becoming more and more like her?*

"Sure thing, Hannah Rush." Sloane grabs Nord's cheeks like she would a chubby baby. "No need to get all crazy."

TWENTY-ONE

ZACH WHITE-KNUCKLES THE STEERING WHEEL.

Going back is risky as hell.

But it was always the plan.

With or without the Administrator. This is no longer about him and his acceptance of things. This is Zach's time. This is Zach Winter connecting the dots.

He feels so stupid.

Hates his weakness.

He so desperately wanted the Administrator's approval, wanted to be seen, heard. But another user has surgically removed that away from him. Carved out his heart with a short video that upstaged all Zach has done.

Everything taken from him in a snap.

The hollow feeling is unbearable. Never experienced anything like it. Never saw it coming. All the emptiness that dominated his world, he thought it gave him strength. Childhood, the constant betrayal of relationships, none of it had prepared him for the depths of this.

Not sure the last time he ate anything. Sleep is a memory. He's running on a different brand of fuel. Heart pumping, thumping, amped by multiple lines of toxic energy.

The truck is silent save for the rolling of the road. The thunder of his thoughts boom and then fade, settling in to that buzz of the hum that resides inside his mind. He's missed it. Been gone too long. That itch where his head and spine collide.

There's an old-school paper map unfolded, spread out beside him along the bench seat of the truck. Couldn't risk a digital footprint off some smart phone map app. He runs his finger along a highway line like veins leading him to a location.

He'll have to be patient.

The game has changed. Taken up a notch.

Monitor, process, access, then wait for that moment that is his and his alone. Not sure when, but he knows he'll know when it presents itself.

Move hard and fast when the time is right. Not a single second before.

No walk-throughs on this. No dress rehearsal.

Tears form at the corners of his eyes, beg to drop. Zach wipes under his nose. Sniffs hard.

"I'm doing this..."

His voice soft and broken.

"I'm doing this for us, Hannah."

TWENTY-TWO

"Where are you?"

Corny's voice is drenched in concern. "Hannah? Please talk to me."

Hannah bites her lip.

Realizes she hasn't talked to her sister since her apartment. A lifetime ago. So much has happened and no way to explain any of it. Corny doesn't know that she met with Nord. Nothing about Sloane or Logan Burke or any of the insanity of what happened in West Texas. No idea about this collective monster living on the internet that Nord talks about.

"Where are you?"

Hannah's mind struggles to find the soft edges of an answer. Thinks maybe she should just dive into the truth. Open up. Let it rip.

Corny will accept it. She'll know what to do. She always does. Hannah's mouth opens, words get stuck in her throat.

She can't do it. She can't tell her.

Can't tell her sister that she's headed to Oklahoma to track down a lead with a journalist who she's pretty sure is lying to her about pretty much everything. And, oh yeah, she's also with a final girl who calls herself Sloane.

You remember that massacre at that corporate retreat a while back?

Yeah, I'm with her. Long story.

"I'm on the road." Hannah looks out across the barren country. An eighteen-wheeler speeds along the highway, blowing her hair back. They'd stopped at a gas station as they crossed over into Oklahoma. Just outside Lawton west of Chickasaw Nation. Wide open land that all looks the same to her. "I can't really say where. But I'm okay."

The silence from her sister's side of the phone is crushing. Hannah can hear her breathing, can feel her searing thoughts even on this end of a call from hundreds of miles away.

"Hannah, I can't help you if you don't talk to me."

"I'm trying to fix this." Hannah's voice booms

more than she wanted. "I can't... I can't say a lot. Believe me, I want to, but I'm being vague for your protection. Sounds like a lie, I know it does, but it's not. I swear to God. The truth is, the less you know, the better."

"*Fix this? My protection?* That's insane. What are you even talking about? Hannah, come back. Come to the house. You can stay here as long as you want. Jake is working with his firm to help—"

"Did Jake send someone to follow me?"

"What?"

"Did Jake's firm send someone? Like he said at my apartment. Did he have like a bodyguard or a private detective or whatever follow me?"

"No. He's got a couple of guys watching your building. They're from a security company the firm has on retainer."

Hannah thinks of the large dead man back in West Texas. Closes her eyes tight. She knew he wasn't from Jake's firm but needed to check that box just to be sure.

Who the hell sent him?

How does Nord know him?

Shakes her head loose from the spiral down. She looks over to Sloane and Nord. Nord is leaning against the truck, working on a fingernail with his teeth. Sloane pumps gas, checking behind her, scanning the highway for threats. Her shirt hangs over a gun Hannah knows is tucked in the back of her jeans. Another one on her hip.

"Well, Jake can probably tell them to take the day off."

"What?"

A sound in the background stops Hannah cold. Luna's soft voice. There's a whisper, then an amazing giggle. Hannah's heart skips a row of beats.

"Can I talk to her?" rushes out of Hannah's mouth before she even thought it.

"What?"

"Can I talk to Luna?"

She feels all her sister's reasons to say *no*. Completely valid, of course. Corny's pause stretches out for what feels like an eternity, then there's a rustle on the phone.

"Han?"

The size of Hannah's smile hurts her face.

She's heard about feeling weightless from being in the orbit of the right person at the exact right moment, but she never knew the jolt of joy that could come from the sound of that right person's voice.

"Hey." She clears her throat, forces herself to sound normal for Luna. "How's it going?"

"I'm good. How are you?"

Hannah's knees weaken. She blinks away a tear.

"I'm good too. Real good. Just traveling a little bit."

"Fun trip? The beach? Are you with your friends?"

"Well..." Hannah glances to Sloane again. She shakes her head, closes her eyes. The lies she's about to tell little Luna stab at her heart. "A little of both, I guess—work and fun—but I'm with some new friends."

"That's good." Luna whispers something to Corny, then comes back. "Are you okay? You sound weird."

"Oh. Do I?" Hannah turns the phone away, coughs hard. "Sorry. No, I'm fine. Just tired from being on the road and all that." Hannah resets. She imagines Corny on the other end trying to listen in for some clues. "Look, Luna, I need to go, but I wanted to tell you that I love you. Okay?" Her voice breaks. "And tell your mom I love her too."

"Love you too, Han."

"Take care of those adults for me, okay?"

"I will."

Hannah hears the shuffle of hands as the phone passes over to Corny. Hannah taps the screen, ending the call. No way she can talk to her sister right now.

No matter how much she wants to.

She'd called Corny to help ease the spiking anxiety, but now she doesn't want the sound of her voice inside her head. At least not any more than it already is. The thought of what she'd say to her, the words she'd use, it burns holes in the center of her mind. That thing in Corny's voice when she's genuinely concerned. When the playful sparring ends and the caring begins. That *hiding under the bed* tone that always let Hannah know the fun and games were over.

"They find him yet?" Sloane is standing behind her.

"Who?" Hannah's shoulders inch up as she turns to face her. "Zach?"

Sloane nods.

"Didn't ask. I'm guessing not or she would have said something."

Sloane goes quiet. Eyes a large SUV that slows down about to turn into the gas station. Her hand drops down, closer to the gun on her hip. Hannah takes note. How she moves. Her first instinct is fight. Sloane stays still, silent until the SUV pulls past, parking in front of the store.

"So." Sloane turns back to Hannah. "You ready for this?"

"For... what exactly?"

Sloane laughs. A cold sort of laugh. Her eyes lock with hers.

Hannah's teeth grind.

"Sorry." Sloane looks to the sky, gathering herself. "Look, you seem like good people. Probably have a nice little job, or *had* a nice little job. Pretty girl. Bet you had a few guys to choose from. Now you've been thrown into something you never even imagined was a vague possibility. *This happens in movies, not to real people*, right? Certainly didn't ask for any of this. Nobody understands that more than me."

"Sloane, I appreciate whatever this is that you're doing—"

"You will never again be who you were. Okay? Never. Get mad, cry, whatever, but when you're done with that, you need to reset your thinking to the simple fact your life will never be the same." Her eyes drift. "Shit like this, it changes everything about you. There's who you were before and then who you are after..." Voice trails off as she places her hand behind her. Hannah knows she's touching the gun tucked in the back of her jeans. Not in a threatening way, more like needing to feel it for comfort. Sloane's eyes stop drifting. "But what we're about to do? What and who we're looking for? You need to get your head right."

"What does that even mean? What are we about to do? Really need everyone to stop talking in bullshit circles and tell me what in the actual hell is going—"

"We are going on a hunt for people. You understand? A hunt for the people responsible for this. And you need to be ready to punch holes into these people. End their lives. Leave their bodies where we drop them." Sloane takes her hand off her gun, eyes burning. "Because that's how this ends. It will not be happy. No warm feeling of accomplishment. This ends in emptiness and blood."

Hannah knows she's right.

Of course she is. In the back of her racing thoughts, Hannah knew this started with a horrible event and would probably end with one was well. An ugly, balanced equation. She looks Sloane over, taking in all that she is. Wonders if they could have been friends before Sloane changed into what she's become. Before Hannah was changed.

"I don't want any of that," Hannah says.

"The luxury of what you want is over. It's their lives or yours. I mean, what's left of your life."

"I'm not like you."

Sloane gives the thinnest smile Hannah has ever seen.

"I'll ask again. Are you ready, Hannah Rush?"

"No."

"Okay." Sloane clucks her tongue, thumbs behind her. "Get your ass in the damn truck anyway."

Without further discussion, Sloane turns and walks away.

PART THREE

TWENTY-THREE

BOBBY GRITS his teeth as he changes lanes.

Pain's still sharp in his shoulder.

No matter. He's been tracking them. They were at a motel off of 87 for a bit, then moved on. Bobby thought that might be where he would get things done. Again, no matter. Their pause has allowed him to make up some much-needed ground.

Checks his phone, letting his knees man the wheel.

The app from his tracking tag indicates they're leaving a gas station about fifteen miles ahead. Bobby puts his hands back on the wheel, presses the pedal down. He knows he'll never catch up no matter how fast he goes, not while they are moving, but he needs to do what he can to shorten the distance between him and them. Keep pace at the very least.

His shoulder has stopped throbbing. Pain's not gone but it has dulled down. Mama's pills worked their magic. Those little wonders also put his mind into a spacey float he's not hating either.

Keeps his grip on the wheel loose.

Turns up Cookie and his Cupcakes. Taps the wheel. Lets his brain drain.

Relives the glow of Dotts_The_Administrator's comment. The high of being the unquestioned king of the board. Imagines what the feed will look like when he finishes this. The scroll will be relentless.

"They're going to lose their fucking minds."

Cranks the tunes up a little louder. His blood nuclear. His mind right.

Final girl and Hannah will stop somewhere. They'll have to. He'll be wherever that is soon enough. Seems like they're headed to Oklahoma. Butterflies flutter in his stomach. The excitement is unbearable.

He needs to take in the moment when it presents itself. Own it. Go all in.

No room for hesitation. Create your chaos, work with what's there no matter when or where.

All his gear is in the trunk. The axe, his chest harness, body armor, the sack. All waiting to come out and play again. Can't remember the last time he's felt this good. He wants this feeling, this moment to last forever.

He's screaming. Didn't know it. Catches the sight of himself in the mirror. Face ruby red. Tears rolling down his face. Life and light practically radiating from him.

So damn happy.

It's disgusting.

He eases his foot off the gas. Slows his roll. Powers off the music. Drives in complete silence. Back stiff. Face void. As if he removed the power to his emotions as well.

The hell you so happy about? Don't get lost in your own bullshit, son.

"Yes, sir."

He rips the dressing away from his shoulder wound, laying the bandage down next to him on the seat. Pulling over on the side of the highway, he jams the car into park.

He looks again into the rearview mirror, locking into himself.

Slaps his gunshot wound over and over again as hard as he can. Bites his lip. Fights not to make a sound. Holds it all in. Accepting what he deserves.

Wipes his eyes. Presses the gauze back onto his shoulder.

Puts the car back in drive, pulling out onto the highway.

TWENTY-FOUR

Nᴏʀᴅ ʜᴀᴅ ɴᴀʀʀᴏᴡᴇᴅ the possible locations to Oklahoma.

Sloane made him show his work.

Hannah listened, did her best to keep Sloane from killing him, thought everything all seemed reasonable based on his explanations, but knew trusting any of it was a big stretch. Sloane, of course, didn't believe a single syllable out of his mouth. Understandable. Hannah hopes that somewhere in the mix the truth might be uncovered.

They'd been at this for a few hours.

Searching. Tracking down the addresses Nord had found.

They climbed wire fences, peeked into

multiple windows of empty businesses, and were chased off the last place by some mean-as-hell dogs. Hannah had to keep Sloane from shooting one of them. She said later she wouldn't actually shoot a dog, just wanted to scare them off, but Hannah still isn't sure. What she does know is if those dogs were people, there would be no question about it—Sloane would have just shot them.

Now, all three of them stand at the last possible location on Nord's list.

A list he says he's been working on for a long time. Nothing on his list has proven to be useful —nothing at all—so things are tilting heavily toward the Sloane school of thought that includes hurting Nord. Badly.

Hannah can tell she's growing more and more impatient with him.

Each time he speaks, the woman's veins pop under her skin. Hannah can't blame her. This guy has spun some serious lies, some tiny crumbs of truth here and there, and has led them around a cluster of small towns in OK with nothing to show for it. After each failed attempt, he'd give a half-assed apology, toss out an excuse of some sort, then they'd move on.

Sloane did hit him after the last place. Hard.

Blackened his eye, then knocked the air out of him with a lightning-quick jab to the gut. Doubled him over as Sloane stood over him. Hannah found it hard to watch but couldn't bring herself to step in. She was done with his bullshit too. Sloane just did what Hannah wasn't willing to do.

Sloane said he had one last chance. That's when he dug deep in his bag, magically finding a new list. One he hadn't shown them before.

That's what brought them here.

"I feel good about this one," Nord chirps. Pausing to absorb their death stares, he lightly touches his blackened eye. "I do."

They are standing in a parking lot, across the street, about hundred yards away from a run-down-looking strip mall.

The whole area is post-apocalyptic in nature. Doors and windows boarded up where businesses used to be. Some didn't even bother with the boards. Windows are smashed with jagged shards of glass still clinging to the frame. Doors barely passing as doors. There is, however, a burger joint that looks to be hanging on at the far end of the strip mall. No, at second glance Hannah sees that it's shut down as well. The green spray-painted *Eat Ass* on the glass is a clear giveaway.

Nord points toward a door on the far side of the strip mall. The windows are unbroken, front door intact. Unlike the rest of the area, it at least looks inhabitable.

"That's it. I can feel it. Trust me on this."

Sloane seethes.

"Why didn't we come here first?" Hannah asks. "If you're so damn sure."

"Well, that's a complicated—"

"Should I have let Sloane beat your ass sooner?"

Nord's eyes bounce between them both.

"Look. We want to be sure, right?" Nord turns back to the strip mall. "Tiny domain company that—according to rumor—pretty much caters to those sites that can't find a home. Doesn't look like much, I know."

Hannah can't even look at him. She can feel the heat rising off Sloane.

"I'll go in and check—" Nord is cut off quick.

Sloane's hand wraps around his throat, stopping him in his tracks.

Hannah digs her shoes into the dirt, ready to jump in if she needs to save him, but wants Sloane to push him a little. Proven to work. Nord has shown he needs motivation other than simply doing the right thing.

"No." Sloane burns. "I'm going in there with you. Hannah will keep an eye out."

Hannah doesn't argue.

Should have done this a long time ago. She'd talked Sloane into giving Nord a little slack to roam with and that was a massive mistake. Never should have trusted anything he's said, but she'd felt they needed to see what he came up with without the violence. When you're out of good options, you sometimes have to do with the bad ones.

Then it occurs to her. She's never seen the actual site. The one that supposedly started this whole thing. Probably her self-defenses kicking in, saving herself by keeping away from scary things. Her eyes are wide open now.

"Show us."

"What?" Nord chokes. "I showed you my notes. This place is credible."

"No." Hannah points to his bag. "Before we go in there, show us the site."

"You sure about that?"

"Yeah..." Sloane releases his throat, leans in to him. "Do it."

Hannah finds it hard to believe Sloane has

never seen it, but maybe she hasn't. Nord swallows hard, then pulls his tablet out from his bag. Sloane scans the area for the hundredth time.

Pulling up the site, he uses a login he claims he paid for using crypto on the dark web. Hannah tells him to access it on her phone as well. Wants to be able to see it on her own without Nord driving the viewing. She holds her breath as he takes them into the site. A guided tour of the place Zach and the Logan Burke worshipers live their digital lives.

It's hard to decipher at first.

Nord explains that the posts expire after a certain amount of time, and again tells them about how not everyone has to pick a username but some do it out of ego, wanting to belong, show off some kind of creativity or whatever. That's what makes it hard to track who's who.

"There has to be a way," Sloane cuts in. "IP addresses or something. Whoever hosts the site has to have a trail to follow."

Nord neither confirms nor denies, saying that's beyond his technical expertise. He also didn't want to stay on the site long. Said he didn't want to draw attention. The Administrator can see when new people are viewing the board if he or she is paying attention. First time Nord had suggested the site might be run by a woman. Seemed unlikely to Hannah but nothing is out of the question right now.

At first, the board seems like fairly harmless stuff—just like Nord had said. People were sharing recipes on some of the pages of the chan. Cocktail mixology stuff. Travel tips and lots of pointed thoughts thrown like daggers about movies and binge-worthy streaming shows. Incredibly tense, heated debates about music. But then Nord shows them another level.

A subhuman level.

They head deeper into the /b/ subforums. Easy to see how someone could tumble down the hole of these political and religious boards. It's like a living, breathing thing that feeds off eyes and minds. All of them flinging rage and bile that seems to be generated by something other than senators and their view of the Lord above.

Not for the faint of heart.

Then, not surprisingly, there's an even uglier side. Racial hate. Kiddy porn. Bomb instructions. Fans cheering school shootings.

There are no rules here. Period.

What Hannah sees makes her want to throw up.

Nord explains this is where some believe free

speech is tested day in and day out. Why some think this site, and others like it, should be protected. If someone truly believes in free speech for all—even if you disagree with the views and opinions expressed, no matter how much the words and images might terrify or disgust you—then this is where that belief is put on trial. A twenty-four-seven Constitutional exercise.

"That's a load of shit," Sloane says.

Hannah nods. Nord decides not to comment. Pushing farther and farther through the subforums, Nord shows them another area.

An invitation-only space.

Nord enters a code that grants them access. Hannah snaps her fingers, wanting the code. Reluctantly, he hands it over. With a shaky hand, she enters the same code on the site on her phone.

They've entered a dark, private hallway on the web.

Filled with even more unbelievable words and memes. The fact that people have nothing better to do with their lives is bad enough, but the fact people take the time to seek out this site and then view, comment, and create this form of trash is too much to accept.

Hannah shakes her head.

Her shock fades with each passing second. Already becoming numb to it all. Never considered herself to be naïve. Not a *cover her mouth in shock grasping her pearls* kind of woman. The world has shown her some of its darkness before but nothing like this.

These pages are just as Nord described it.

A tiny spot on the world wide web filled with people devoted to the ideas and legend of Logan Burke. Kneeling at the digital altar. All seeking his approval. There're links to stories about him. Multiple pics of the corporate retreat in the woods. Graphic crime scene photos. Blood. Bodies.

Hannah looks to Sloane. These are friends, people she knew. Sloane's expression does not break. Does not look away.

There's an undeniable need for attention that seeps from the pages of the site. It's deep in the words used. The way people phrase everything. Everyone trying to outdo one another. Each of them desperate to be heard. To be seen by their hero.

A guy who murdered in order to satisfy some twisted, unexplainable need. What this man did spoke to these people on the site on some sad, pathetic level. Post after post. Line after line.

Anger doesn't cover it. This is something more primitive than *anger*.

There's constant calling, begging for violence. Violence against women in particular. Describing it as misogynist doesn't do it justice. Cartoons of rape. Beheadings. A GIF of Sloane being dragged behind a truck by her throat. Another of her bent over a kitchen island while something that looks a horned demon grins behind her.

None of this seems to surprise Sloane at all.

She watches on in complete silence, as if she is looking at content she's seen many, many times before. Simply a review of what is already known.

Hannah admires and fears Sloane's detachment from the pages that light up the screen. She knew she needed to look at all this garbage with an analytical eye, but now that it's in front of her? She never wants to be that removed from being human. Never wants to see things like this and feel nothing.

She thinks of things Sloane has said to her.

Hannah knows she's not prepared to become like them in order to hunt them, although she understands that's exactly how Sloane views it all. Sloane needs the content. Thinks she needs it for fuel. She's probably not wrong.

Suddenly, Hannah grabs Nord by the throat.

Feels good. Right. Squeezes hard, wanting to see his eyes pop open like windows into fear. Her blood burns hot. Those faceless people on that site. All the things that Nord isn't telling them. He deserves this and so much more.

"Hannah. Please." Nord tugs and slaps at her hand. "Listen."

She releases him and stumbles back. Face slacks down into a void, disbelief of what she did. It came on so fast. Complete loss of control. Went out of body in a blink.

"Seen enough. We get it." Sloane checks her gun, unfazed by what just happened. "Let's go."

"Hey." Nord fights to find his breath. "Going in with guns blazing is not going to get us what we need."

Hannah steps away, working to gather herself.

"This isn't up for debate." Sloane musses Nord's hair. *Silly boy.* "I'm going in there with you. You can start, ask them whatever, but if I feel that you're holding back? Hiding something..." Shows her gun. "I'm joining the conversation."

"I agree." Hannah keeps her voice even and calm. "I'm going in too. I want to hear everything." Sloane coils, about to bark. Hannah stops her. "There's one goal. Go in there, come out with useable information. No matter how small."

Sloane gets in Hannah's face. "You need to stay out here. You're not ready for any of—"

"I'm not looking to debate it." Hannah pushes her fear down. Showing none of it. "We need information. We are not going in there to hurt someone for the sake of hurting someone."

"Funny coming from the chick who almost choked a dude out a few seconds ago." Not requiring a response, Sloane turns and moves toward the strip mall.

"Come on." Hannah pushes Nord forward as if he were a lazy teenager. "This is your time to shine, buddy."

"I'm not hiding anything from you." He coughs. "I swear to God I'm not."

"Better not. Pretty sure one of us will kill you."

"I said there were leads around here, not stone-cold truths. I'm trying here."

Hannah stops walking, puts her hands on Nord's shoulders.

"I don't trust you. Not at all. This is your last chance to help yourself." Hannah points to Sloane up ahead of them. "I'm sorry I lost it. I am. But never forget, she's not sorry about hurting you. Not at all. I don't want to kill you, but the idea of you being in pain is growing on me. If you are hiding something, protecting something or someone, now is the time to come clean."

Hannah stare zeros in.

"I've been nothing but straight with both of you."

Hannah raises her eyebrows. *That's some serious bullshit.*

"Well." Nord resets. "I've been truthful when it counts."

The Oklahoma winds blows around them. Hannah lets the disarming quiet fill the space between them, hopefully creating some doubts in Nord's mind. Perhaps some fear. Hell, even a bit of guilt would be nice.

Nord's expression never changes. Not the slightest hint of anything. His almost unbreakable smugness is on full display. Hannah found it vaguely charming in the beginning, but now she can't stand it. She doesn't know the extent of his lies, but she's convinced Sloane is right about one thing.

Nord is lying about almost everything.

But can I even trust Sloane?

Is the gun I'm carrying the only thing keeping the peace between us? Will Sloane bounce out of sanity and kill me after she kills Nord?

Hannah's popcorn thoughts bounce. Paranoia taking hold.

Is Sloane playing out some private agenda that I can't see yet?

One I can't even understand?

Hannah hates thinking like this. This circular, almost never-ending spiral of fear that climbs up and over, fueled by its own momentum. Will she always be looking over her shoulder? Never able to sleep. She can't remember the last time she laughed, let alone felt comfortable in her own skin.

Her phone buzzes.

Pulling it from her pocket, she sees that 512 number on the screen yet again.

And once again, she taps it away.

The same number litters her missed calls list. The relentless nature of robocalls or whatever blah-blah homecare service has become almost comforting. Something she can trust. She smirks, thinking it's one of the few things she can depend on.

She pockets her phone, then checks her gun.

"Nord." Hannah puts her arm around Nord, walking them toward Sloane and the blown-out strip mall. "You should probably treat this like you're auditioning for your life."

TWENTY-FIVE

THE DOOR CHIMES A DYING DING.

An overweight man sits at a desk surrounded by monitors, computers, and empty fast food remains. What little hair he has spikes in every direction, held in place by what Hannah assumes is greasy despair. There's a desk tent that reads *This is Chad's World, Bitch.*

Sloane is first through the door.

Chad sits up, brushing off snack debris from his black T-shirt. Sucks his Cheeto-stained fingers. Obviously taken aback by the fact anyone is here, let alone that a female is anywhere near him.

"Yeah. Hey..." Chad coughs up a lung. "Can I help you?"

Hannah and Nord step inside as Sloane moves in closer to Chad.

"I know you, right?" Chad shoves his chin towards Nord.

Nord's eyes pop wide. Hannah wants to kill him. Sloane is way ahead of her. Pulling her gun, she whips the barrel around, slamming it across Nord's face, putting him down on the ground. She pulls his tablet from his bag, then rages toward Chad.

"Hey, lady, I don't know what the hell—"

Sloane jams the barrel of her gun between Chad's eyes, then slams the tablet down on the table.

"Who runs this site?" Sloane barks.

Hannah watches, heart pounding. This could slip out of control fast.

"What?" He glances to the tablet. Shakes his head. "I can't tell you that." Voice cracks.

Sloane takes a step back, then kicks him in the face. His chunky body jolts. Head snaps back into the wall before he slumps down to the left. Inches from spilling out to the floor.

Sloane pulls her fist back.

Chad holds his hands up, begging for a moment. Eyes pleading. "I can't tell you. It's the only reason why I have customers. They can't go anywhere else. If I tell you—"

Sloane kicks him again, this time putting him on the floor. She picks up the tablet. Using her knees to pin his arms down, she shoves the tablet's glass into his face.

"Who runs this shit?"

"Sloane," Hannah calls out.

"I can't tell you. I swear. Please."

She tosses the tablet at Nord.

"Sloane!"

Sloane reaches back, fires a point-blank bullet into Chad's thick thigh. He screams out in agony. She keeps her knees on his arms, pinning him down. Thrashing side to side with everything he has, he desperately tries to grab his leg. She won't let him.

Hannah shoves Sloane free. Diving into her, they tumble to the side in a heap.

Chad holds his leg. His sobs roll into screaming cries for help that's not coming.

Sloane spins away from Hannah, coming up with her gun raised. Hannah has her gun leveled on Sloane. Both hold their aim, breathing in and out between clenched teeth.

Nord makes a break for the door.

Sloane fires two shots above his head, putting

him down on his knees covering his head with his hands. In a single motion, her gun's back on Hannah.

"Stop!" Hannah screams.

"I told you how this was going to end, Hannah. Them or us."

"I'm not going to stand back and watch you—"

"Then don't watch."

Sloane moves back to Chad. She puts the gun to his temple.

"Tell her," Hannah says, pleading in her voice. "She'll do it. I might not be able to stop her again."

Chad's red, tear-filled eyes dance between Sloane and Hannah. Sloane presses the gun harder to the side of head. Body trembling, his face now pressed against the floor.

"Is it in Oklahoma?" Hannah pleads.

Chad closes his eyes.

"Is it?" Sloane barks.

He manages a nod.

Hannah gets to her feet, scrambling to the mess spread across the desk, searching frantically to find a pen and something to write on. She shoves a used hamburger wrapper and a pen into his hand.

"Write down the address," Hannah says. "Do it now."

Chad's eyes burn. Hannah can see the war waging inside of him.

"This is wrong," he says. "This is against everything—"

"Stop talking." Sloane's words are like ice. "Do what you're told."

"Do it and we'll call you an ambulance," Hannah reassures him. "They'll fix your leg up. You'll be okay."

Chad breathes in deep, sits up against the wall, then presses the wrapper to the floor and scribbles out an address.

"Verify it's real," Sloane tells Hannah. "Not a random bank, burger barn or some shit."

Hannah takes the wrapper, mapping the address on her phone. Only a few miles away but looks to be way out in the country. A residence, maybe. Secluded. She rushes over to Nord. Slides on her knees, shoving the phone in his face.

"This look right, asshole?"

Nord eyes the screen. Face drops as he tries to form words. He doesn't have to say anything.

"This is it," Hannah calls back to Sloane.

"Good."

Sloane pulls the trigger. The blast booms, rolling into a haunting echo.

Chad's body slumps down to the floor. Mist where half his head should be.

"Thank you for that, Hannah."

Hannah is frozen, only the slamming of her heart tells her this is real.

"Thanks for the good cop, bad cop."

Sloane walks out the door.

TWENTY-SIX

A SMALL, ranch-style home sits nestled between small clusters of trees up ahead.

Next to it, connected by a path made of flat stones, is a silver barn with a red front door that shines under the sun. Looks to be made of a mix of aluminum and steel, with a small window on each side, blinds closed tight.

A massive, matte-black Ford Raptor and a lime-green Land Rover are parked in the grass in front of the house. Hannah can't help but think of the lords of new tech money who roam the streets of Austin. Young, disposable income slaves with no idea of who they are, so they buy cars that—as social media explains—they identify with as a person.

The pang of her life in Austin hits her.

She hadn't thought about her apartment, her job, any part of her days and nights in A-town in what seems like forever. Hannah leans on Sloane's truck, digging through the bag she packed in her apartment. Her *go-bag* before she had a clue what a go-bag was or where she was going.

No real reason to look in her bag, she just felt the need to look through her things. Feel grounded to her life again maybe. Her clothes are still balled and stuffed in. Her bottle of vodka now no longer a chilled delight. Her favorite knife. The card Nord gave her. She almost laughs out loud as she reads the back: *There's a lot you need to know, Hannah.*

No shit, Nord.

Then she comes to something that stops her cold. Something that was so shocking at the time but is now only an odd curiosity.

She runs her fingers over the envelope from her father.

One like the one Corny received, and her mother, and was told to give to her. Still unopened. Contents still a guess. Hannah completely forgot it was in there. Her mind has been swallowed whole, taken in by everything that's happened. Everything that has led them to this place, to whatever terror she's about to face over the coming hours. Perhaps minutes.

Nord's hands are zip-tied to the steering wheel.

The keys to the truck have been removed.

He will not be joining them. Trust and the selfless help of Nord are not reliable concepts at the moment. Hannah is more than a little surprised Sloane didn't kill him and leave him with Chad. Maybe she feels there's still information to mine from him. He was threatened within an inch of his life on the way here. Sloane slapped him around, asking how Chad knew him while Hannah gripped the wheel and chewed on the inside of her cheek. Not liking it, but not stopping it either. He gave them nothing. Retreated inward, staying silent no matter what Sloane did or said. A shell of the guy Hannah met in the laundry room of her building.

Hannah doesn't know if Nord will ever be of use.

She doesn't know much. Her ears still ring like hell from when Sloane killed Chad. The image of the mist of blood pluming from his torn-apart head forever seared into her mind. Sloane did it so easily. Without a thought or a moment of pause. Hannah can't help but be envious of her no matter how brutal her actions. Jealous of how Sloane can glide in and out of these horrible things.

She's right, Hannah thinks. *I'm not ready for this.*

A person never knows how they are going to react in certain moments. Most people see themselves as the star in the big-time action movie. Shooting, jumping, moving, and saying clever things at the right time. But Hannah is almost certain she's not any of that. She might be clever at times, but she's not a killer.

She's been pushed to the edge recently, closer than she ever thought imaginable.

Can only guess that killing someone is another thing that changes you forever. There's everything before, then everything after.

"You didn't have to do that," Hannah says.

"Do what?" Sloane is surveying the house up ahead through a rifle scope she must have removed from one of her many guns. Studying every inch. Scanning left and right, pausing at certain points, then moving on.

"Kill him." Hannah rubs her face. "You didn't have to kill that guy. He gave us what we wanted. He told us about this place."

"Oh? So you don't think he would have

contacted whoever is in that house?" Sloane's eyes never leave her target. "Don't think he might reach out to someone who might wish us harm? Maybe do a fun, snarky, highly informative post on the board that put us here in the first place?"

Hannah starts to say something, then stops. Hates it, but knows Sloane is right. Part of her doesn't want to admit she's glad Sloane did what she did. Thankful, even. She squeezes her eyes closed tight. Shakes her head.

Is this how it starts?

The micro-compromises.

The rationalizations that multiply and spread until you've become something you don't recognize. If you passed your old self on the street, would you even know who it was? There's no question Hannah wants this to end, but at what cost? And will it truly stop here? Even if they kill everyone in that house, will that even make the slightest difference? Is the world too broken to even pretend to care?

"What do you think is in there?" she asks Sloane.

"Not sure." Sloane checks the load, slips one gun behind her back, then checks the other clicked into her hip holster. "Could be everything, or nothing."

A chill runs down Hannah's spine.

We could die in there.

This could be the end of everything. A fact so damn obvious that she'd blocked it from her wandering mind. Thoughts tumble and burn. A flash of Corny's face when they were kids. Her mother's beautiful face in the sun at a picnic at a park. The good. Not a single frame of the bad. She lands on a favorite memory of Luna. The details tear through her. It was when she was two —maybe not even that—and little Luna tumbled over to Hannah with a mouthful of Goldfish crackers and the most amazing light in her eyes. Luna grabbed Hannah's cheeks, then in the sweetest voice she's ever heard or ever will hear, she said that she loved Han.

Simple magic of a child's words.

No agenda. Nothing to gain. An unfiltered expression of the only thing that matters. Hannah wipes away her rolling tear before Sloane can see it.

"Check your gun." Sloane is back to scoping the house.

Hannah forces herself free from her memories. Needs her head in the right place.

"I'm not asking you to kill. Okay?" She turns to Hannah, hint of concern in her gaze. First sign of human emotion Hannah has seen from her. "We share something. Something we have in common. It's broken and unwanted, but it is ours. And we're the only ones left alive who share this very specific, very horrific experience."

Hannah feels a lump in her throat rob her of words.

"So." Sloane looks down, avoiding eye contact. "I'm only asking you to protect us in there."

Hannah knows there's a slim difference between *kill* and *protect* in this situation but understands the distinction. The only way out of this, the only path to some form of a normal life, is behind those walls up ahead.

"Can you do that?" Sloane checks the tactical blade strapped to her ankle. "Will you at least give me that?"

A blistering calm engulfs Hannah.

"I'll give you that."

TWENTY-SEVEN

SLOANE AND HANNAH circled the home the best they could.

The open land with only a spattering of trees and brush made it challenging to move undetected. Slow. Deliberate. Every step thoughtful.

They made note of the entrances and exits. Potential points of failure.

Wanted to get a good look at the layout of what they were walking into. Wanted to understand the barn's place in all this. Sloane spoke low and in technical terms that Hannah barely understood, but apparently the electrical system leading into the barn, along with the gas-powered backup generators, indicated the barn could be used to house servers and whatever else might run this provider of last resort.

Made sense. Tracked.

The longer they're here, the more Hannah can feel the bubbling rage radiate from Sloane. They know in their bones this is the place. This might not complete the puzzle, but it has the look of one massive piece. She wonders if Nord knew about this house all along. Tries to rationalize, parse out how much he's been holding back.

Are there personal reasons? Has he been threatened?

But in the end, there's nothing that excuses how he's so casually covered the depth of his understanding of all this.

What's his game?

He's obviously a writer with a deadline who's dragging the weight of a big cash advance that he can't pay back. Sloane has confirmed that much, and what Hannah could find on the internet about him seems to sync up with that. Still, it doesn't all connect. Maybe there's a few even larger puzzle pieces Nord has hidden for his own benefit.

But what are they, and more importantly, why?

Hannah and Sloane have settled on a spot just inside a group of trees.

Provides them some cover but also allows

them a view of the front of the house and the barn. No signs of life so far. Zero movement that could be seen through the windows. No lights turned on, no flickers of televisions. But the fact there are two vehicles parked out front indicates someone is inside.

The waiting is killing her.

The rising anxiety of anticipation vibrates deep down. This complete absence of control is crushing her. Acceptance of how little control she has right now isn't coming easy. She's entrenched in a reactionary stance. The forced act of pause, sit, then respond when violence and death come raining down isn't sitting well with her.

To call it *unnatural* is a colossal understatement.

She was asked to protect Sloane—and herself —and promised she would. She glances to Sloane. Jaw clenched tight the way she does. Muscles coiled under her tattooed skin. The fact she asked Hannah to protect herself indicated some sign of caring.

Is that all that's left inside Sloane? A dim, flickering sign of caring about another human being?

Hannah thinks about the metal house in

West Texas. Of what she did there. How she stared down a killer. Mind buzzing, circling a single idea, gaining ground on the inevitable inch by inch—that might have been the moment she moved closer to being Sloane.

Hannah had moved without fear. Without hesitation.

Not the same person she was only days ago. No hint of the woman who sat in a cubical each day waiting to sink into her bathtub and drink away the day. Her past methods of controlling her world seem ridiculous, teenage girl-like in comparison.

Then it hits her. She did have control.

In West Texas, with the killer, control wasn't hers, certainly not at first. But she got it. When the time came, the moment that control of her life was threatened, she took it. Grabbed it by the throat. Made it hers.

When she ended her marriage.

When she refused to open the envelope from a father who'd abandoned her.

When those detectives wanted nothing more than to manipulate her.

Hannah took back what she could control.

A warm wave washes over her. Maybe it's self-soothing thoughts clouding up reality, but she can't help it. This feels good. As crazy as it sounds, despite what the future may have in store for her, she cannot hold back the smile spreading across her face. Completely the wrong time for a breakthrough in personal growth, but she doesn't care.

Her smile drops as a new, penetrating idea stabs at her.

Will I have the strength to do it when it matters the most?

Easy to cherry-pick the best moments in life, but there's more than a few examples where Hannah had fumbled and flailed.

She looks again to Sloane.

The scars, the weapons, the amazing emotional walls constructed by violence and harm. Is that *Sloane's way* of dealing with it all? Her choice of how to handle the life that's been forced upon her. Hannah's head swirls. Too much to carve up right now.

She works her breathing the way the therapist preached.

Thinks of Corny holding her hand under the bed.

Sees Luna giggle and grin in her mind's eye. Wants to place that snapshot image on a mantle in her soul and—

Sloane hooks Hannah's arm, spinning them both behind a tree.

A wiry guy—late twenties, early thirties maybe—steps out from the house wearing black sweats and no shirt. Rubs his long, wild hair like a lion's mane. Looks like he might have just woken up. Yawns huge, cup of coffee in hand. Tats decorate him from his jaw to his waistline. He unlocks the barn's red door and slips the key somewhere into his sweats.

They look to the house, wanting to see any sign of more people inside. Zero movement. No TV left on. Not a sound.

Satisfied that he's alone at the house, Sloane nods to Hannah as she flips the magnetic strap of her hip holster open. Hannah readies her gun. Breathes in deep. Mind buzzes.

Following Sloane's lead, they move in, staying low. Sloane told her earlier that *slow is smooth and smooth is fast*. Working a slow pattern toward the barn, they do their best to stay clear of the sight lines. The windows are still covered but any quick, jarring moves outside might draw the eyes of those inside. Sloane said once they breached the door they needed to operate with *speed and violence*.

Reaching the side of the barn, they crouch down.

They'd briefly outlined a plan while they waited for a sign of life from the house. To call it a plan is a loose statement at best, but the goal is to go in hard and find out everything this guy knows. Most importantly: who is behind the board; who is the administrator; how to shut it all down.

Sloane checks her load one last time.

Hannah does the same. Her heart thumps hard against her ribs. Throat dry.

Sloane raises her eyebrows, looking for a green light.

Hannah knows that everything that happens next, happens fast.

TWENTY-EIGHT

Sloane and Hannah charge the red door.

Sloane kicks at the steel once, then twice, with Hannah alternating with her own kicks in between.

The door jolts and clangs before giving way.

Pushing inside, they keep their guns tracking the corners, scanning the open areas, stopping as their hard eyes find who they want.

The wiry guy stands surrounded by equipment and stacks of servers flashing greens and reds. He's inches away from a shotgun resting on a rack near the window.

"Stop!" Sloane booms.

She makes long, quick strides toward him, her gun leveled on his face.

The wiry guy's eyes pop wide, every muscle in his body seizing. Hannah rushes over, slipping the shotgun from his fingertips, then sends it skidding across the concrete floor to the far corner. Away from them and the front door.

"What the hell?" the wiry guy spits. Hints of an Eastern European accent cling to his words.

Sloane presses her gun to his forehead, pushing him to a desk in the middle of the barn filled with monitors, an open laptop, and multiple smartphones. Clean. Everything orderly, in its right place. Hannah holds her gun with two hands, alternating back and forth between him and the door.

"Show him," Sloane says to Hannah.

Hannah taps, finds the site, then shoves her phone's screen into to Wiry Guy's face, making him look at the site. A clear view of the board that Zach and the others worship. He looks at the screen, then back at Hannah, then Sloane. Disbelief and confusion own his face.

Finally, recognition lights up behind his dark eyes.

"Holy fucking shit. It's you," he sneers. "Look at you two. Hannah Rush and Final Girl. Here. You are both actually here in—"

Sloane cracks the side of his knee. Drops him down to the floor.

Hannah's hands start to shake. She sets the gun down, shakes them back, then grips the gun.

He knows us.

Every part of her starts to burn. This is it. This place is so much more than a piece of the puzzle. This could be it. The end of everything. She slams her phone down on the desk and drops down to the floor. Leans into his face.

"Who runs the site?" Hannah shoves the gun barrel into his eye. Didn't know she did it until after she heard him gasp. Face twisted in pain and shock. "Who is the Administrator?"

He snorts a half-laugh.

"Asshole." She removes the gun from his eye, slapping him across the face with the barrel. Moving on instinct. Something else has taken over her. "We will kill you, but not before we hurt you." Hannah stands up. A voice in the back of her mind screams, begs for her to take a breath. "Talk to us. Who runs the site?"

He laughs harder.

She looks to Sloane. She can't believe Sloane hasn't started taking this piece of shit apart yet. Sloane stands staring, looking at something on the desk. Wiry Guy keeps laughing, but now points at the desk. At the monitor that has all of Sloane's attention.

Onscreen is the site.

The board is alive and active. Streaming with posts. Buzzing like a beehive.

Hannah leans closer. There's a live stream in progress.

Hannah recognizes the images. It's the house outside. The metal barn comes into view. The username *Better_thanyour_Better* is showing a shaky cam shot broadcasting in real time.

Sloane moves to a window, peeking through the blinds.

"Anything?" Hannah whisper-barks.

Sloane shakes her head as she moves to the only other window. Wiry Guy keeps laughing, blood seeping from a cut above his eye.

"Shut the hell up." Hannah turns back to the screen.

The live stream seems to be coming from where she and Sloane were waiting earlier, standing in the trees. Hannah's heart jumps up into her throat. She snaps her fingers at Sloane, then points at the screen. A shoulder has come into frame.

Sloane glances over to her, then the screen.

"There are two of them," Hannah says.

"At least."

"You're so fucked." Wiry Guy's almost bursting with joy. "I mean, I've got no dog in this fight—just a fanboy over here trying to turn a dime into a dollar."

"Told you to shut up, man." Hannah looks back and forth between him and the screen,

thinking, but her thoughts ignite and burn away as soon as they form.

"Can't believe I've got the best seat in the whole damn house. They're going to make me part of the story now."

"What?" Hannah turns all her attention to him. "What story?"

"All this..." He pushes himself up on his elbows. "The greatest show on earth, all being directed by the Administrator himself."

Her eyes slip to the screen. The cam is still outside in the trees. They are waiting. Maybe surveying the area just like they did earlier. The camera jars back and forth. Sloane points to the bottom of the screen. Comments roll under the video.

Gut those fucking bitches.

Show those sluts how shit gets done.

Then *Better_thanyour_Better* comments. *Soon bruthas.*

Hannah feels a click in her head as something inside her unhinges.

She shoots Wiry Guy in the knee.

He screams out in pain, twisting and thrashing on the floor. The booming echo rattles off the metal walls. Hannah and Sloane both look to the screen. The cam outside has stopped moving. The comments have slowed to almost nothing. Only a trickle of hate now.

The last one asking, *was that a gunshot?*

"Yes it was, bitch." Hannah keeps her gun on Wiry Guy. Looks to Sloane. "What now?"

Sloane rushes over to the window, again checking every angle.

"I can't see anybody." Sloane comes back over, standing next to Hannah.

They both look at the screen. The live stream has stopped. Only a black box where the video was seconds ago.

"You think that scared them off?" Hannah looks to the door.

Sloane doesn't answer, turning her attention to Wiry Guy. She bends down, and without hesitation, jams her finger into the bullet wound. He screams even louder. A higher level of pain unlocked. Face red. Veins popping. Hannah cringes but doesn't stop the tactic. Can't lie to herself that's she's just a passive lamb in all this. Part of her enjoys his pain. The other part is horrified by how much she does.

"Are you the Administrator?" Sloane cocks her head. Cold and calm.

He keeps wailing. Sweat pours. She pushes deeper.

"Are you?"

"No... No! Please stop!"

Sloane pulls away from his wound. Wipes her finger clean across his chest.

"Then who the fuck is?"

"I don't know." Wiry Guy's skin has gone white, face drained. Fights to get words out between the cries. "I swear to God. Never met him. Only phone calls. No names. A bank account. Probably a bullshit shell company. Please, you have to believe—"

"But you know something about a show, right?" Sloane moves her hand over his trembling knee. "You talked about a show."

"No." He jumps back like a wounded animal. "He said he would give me a piece of something big if I hosted the site. Ran the tech. Talked about a big show with all kinds of shit."

"Is it Nord?" Hannah asks.

"Told you, don't know a name."

"Is it Logan Burke?"

"What? That's a myth." He points to the monitor. "A freakshow fantasy."

Hannah turns left and right in quick jerks looking for something that might tell them something. She stops at the desk behind them.

"This laptop?" She thumbs back to the desk. "Those portable hard drives that look like they could survive a missile strike. All these damn phones. It's possible that somewhere in all that hardware, buried in all that shit, we'll find what we want to know?"

He breathes in and out through gnashed teeth.

"Talk to me or we're going knee-digging again."

Sloane shoves Hannah's hand away. Places the tip of her finger on his wound.

"Yes. Okay goddamit, yes there is—"

His sentence ends. His eyes pop wild and wide. But not from pain.

Sloane and Hannah spin around.

Nord's body is shoved through the door. It slaps the floor like a side of beef, bouncing off the concrete. He lies still. Blood flows out from his throat like a river.

Hannah and Sloane stand with guns raised. Hearts pounding.

Motion on the monitor catches Hannah's attention. The black box has filled back up with pixilated video. The live stream has started again. The camera image blurs, whipping around and showing Hannah and Sloane.

A man with a sack over his head and slits cut for the mouth and eyes storms through the door. Axe in his thick hands, he charges hard at Sloane.

Sloane opens fire. One shot blasts wide, the second lands in his chest. He barely pauses.

Hannah fires but misses. Bullets zip over his head as he dives, slamming into Sloane.

They tumble to the ground in a twisted mess of arms and legs. The man tries to jam the axe under her chin. Sloane lands the butt of her gun to his jaw.

The axe hits the floor.

She pulls the trigger.

Bobby Greene slaps her hand away and the bullet thunks the metal roof. Punches, kicks, and clawing fingers rage as they flip and roll. Sloane's gun skids a few feet away.

Hannah struggles to find a clean shot.

From the corner of her eye, she sees Wiry Guy scrambling on all fours toward the back corner of the barn. Heading for the shotgun, streaking a trail of blood as he goes.

"No!" she screams, leveling her gun on him.

Wiry Guy flips over on his back with the shotgun raised. Hannah opens fire. Bullets burst open pops of flesh across his body as stray shots punch holes into the metal walls.

As she turns back to the fight, a fat fist lands, putting her down.

The back of her heard bounces off the concrete floor. Everything goes silent in the world for a blink. Her eyes flicker, white blurs growing, crowding out her sight. Brain lost in a dense fog.

She can taste her blood as it rolls down her throat. Fights to hold on to consciousness as it blinks in and out. He stands over her. Axe raised with one arm. Sack still covering his face as it sucks in and out with his heaving breaths. Time slows to a crawl.

She can see the phone that's been clicked into some sort of harness on his chest, strapped onto his ballistic vest. A tattered hole where Sloane shot him.

Her fingers scramble, looking for a weapon, but her hands find nothing. The gun must have fallen with the punch. Looking into the lens of the camera, she realizes her death will be televised.

This is what he wants.

What they all want.

He hasn't lowered the axe on her yet because he's savoring the moment. His moment.

"Zach is better than you," she says, spitting blood along with her words. Said it loud so the fans could hear her too. "So much better."

She can see the anger building between the slit cut for his eyes. He raises the axe higher, grunts as he grabs it with both hands.

Hannah kicks her heel into his knee with everything she has.

A loud, cracking pop sounds. Ligaments forced in a direction they were never designed to go. The man yelps, muffled by the mask. The axe comes down in a weak, uncontrolled swing, clanging on the concrete floor as Hannah spins clear.

She can only manage to pull herself up onto her knees. *Move, Hannah.* Using the palms of her hands, pushing off with the balls of her feet, she forces herself to crawl to the back corner of the barn. Off balance, the entire world seems to tilt left and then right as she gets to her feet. Fumbling, falling, but always moving forward, she staggers toward the shotgun waiting in Wiry Guy's lap.

A thick hand grabs her ankle, pulling her back down.

Her hands slap the concrete. She pushes off the floor, twisting her hips enough to land a foot to his face.

He adjusts the grip, moving up her leg. She can see he has her gun in his hand as he levels the weapon on her. She kicks three hard, fast kicks like a jackhammer to his face.

His grip releases.

She drags herself to the shotgun. Pulling it free, she turns, squeezing the trigger.

Nothing happens.

Squeezes it again. Nothing.

A box of shells lies next to Wiry Guy's body. He'd been trying to load it.

Everything inside of Hannah falls away. She's lost. They've won.

The man laughs like a little child.

Hannah doesn't have to look at the screen. She can see the comments stacking up in her mind. The misplaced hate. The underserved, unearned rage about their place in the world. The memes. *Bitch. Whore.* One after another and on and on.

Han tried.

She hopes Luna will do better.

The man laughs louder.

Hannah stares into the phone's lens. She gives them the finger.

The laugh stops abruptly. As if a string was pulled.

The man twitches, thrashes from side to side. Body heaves and jerks. Hard, choking coughs explode from his lips. Spit flies from the sack. As he turns, Hannah sees Sloane standing behind him with the axe in her hands.

Blade slick with blood.

She looks beaten, drained of life. Eyes distant. Hair matted with her own blood.

Hannah sees a massive gash near the man's spine.

Sloane drops to her knees, wilts to the floor. Used up whatever she had left to swing the axe.

The man lunges at her.

Hannah launches herself toward the man. She swings the butt of the shotgun, slamming it into the side of his head. The man lands on his stomach. Hannah's blood burns. She feels out of body, as if she's watching herself.

The man tries to push off the floor, lands on his back.

Hannah picks up the axe from Sloane, then stands over him.

He reaches for the gun next to him.

"Don't." Grips, lifts the axe. "Please don't."

She thinks how Sloane wouldn't have hesitated. She'd plant this axe into his head without a hint of a warning. No moment of mercy. She's not sure that's *not* the right thing to do right now.

The man coughs, fingers still searching. He'll have the gun soon.

Axe raised, Hannah's mercy wearing thin.

The man's arm jerks forward. Hannah brings the blade down with all that she has. The axe's blade digs into his throat and collarbone. Blood erupts from his mouth. A spray rips across her face. He squeezes the trigger. A harmless bullet zips a few feet from her head.

Hannah looks into the phone's lens, then turns to the screen on the desk.

She can see herself on the screen. A different version of herself. One she doesn't recognize or want to. Covered in blood. Eyes hard and softly drifting at the same time.

Watching the man's body spasm before fading into stillness.

Her shoulders drop. She looks into the lens and thinks of all those lost souls watching. All staring breathless at their screens, feeding off hate-fueled bloodlust.

Hannah waves goodbye, then removes the phone from the harness.

Taps out her own comment.

Fuck you.

TWENTY-NINE

HANNAH SLIDES DOWN NEXT to Sloane, who lies motionless on the floor.

Hannah checks her pulse the best she can, pressing her fingers to her neck. A flood of relief rushes through her. Weak, but there's the faint bump of life.

"Got to get you out of here." Hannah eyes the door. Forms a plan of how to reach the truck. "Just hang on. Stay with me. You hear me?"

Nothing from Sloane.

Hannah holds the back of her hand to her mouth. Looking. Spinning. She springs toward the desk, grabs her phone, finger raised and poised to tap out 9-1-1.

She stops.

Think.

They are out in the middle of nowhere but not far from a small town. They'd seen another house down the road in the middle of some land. Drove through some shopping areas a few miles before that. There has to be a hospital or some emergency clinic near here.

She paces, trying to get her head around what's happened. Sloane doesn't have much time. Hannah needs to make the right decision fast.

Those booming gun blasts would be hard to ignore, even out in the wilds of Oklahoma.

Police will come. Probably soon if they aren't already on the way.

She works to figure out what she would say to the police that might be there any second. She thinks of the detectives who visited her in her apartment.

They'd wanted to pin something on her. Wanted to find a way to blame her for all of this. They would have done anything to wrap up the case right then and there. She sees the card that Detective Huston gave her still stuck in the pocket on her phone case.

Will these police do the same? Will they even try to listen to me?

Think.

FOR YOU

Sloane needs help or she'll die on this floor.

That's not going to happen.

Ideas slosh through her muddy mind, trying to apply reason and logic to what's laid out in front of her.

The bodies. The blood. The tech.

It hits her. *The tech.* Sloane thought there might be a way to track these people. A jumping-off place. She spots a black trash bag next to a shredder.

Moving with manic, frantic energy, she grabs the bag. Shoves in whatever she can. The laptop, the portable hard drives, a handful of thumb drives, the phones. She ties off the bag and drags it over next to Sloane.

Sirens wail in the distance.

"Shit."

She thinks of Sloane telling her to wipe down the motel. There's no time. No way to even begin to go through everything she's touched in this barn. And there is so much more than fingerprints to worry about here.

Think.

Takes a few tries, but Hannah manages to get Sloane up using her arm over her shoulder wounded-soldier style. Sloane's eyes flicker and fade, but she still finds a way to help by moving her legs, supporting her body the best she can. Walking, dragging each other along, Hannah throws the trash bag over her shoulder.

"That was pretty cool, right?" Sloane whispers.

Hannah can't help but laugh. "Shut up."

The truck isn't too far up the road. The sirens still seem to be far away but impossible to tell. The wide-open space and wind make it difficult to judge sound. The flat land, however, makes visibility easy. Shouldn't be hard to spot any police cruisers screaming their way.

Fighting for every step, sharp pain in every breath, they push and pull one another to the truck. Hannah helps Sloane up and into the passenger side, then hobbles around behind the wheel, setting the trash bag between them. She turns the key, cranking up the old but reliable-as-hell truck. A V8 engine has never sounded so sweet.

Pops it in drive.

As they begin to roll forward, Hannah looks to her phone, tapping out directions to the nearest medical facility. There's something about ten miles from here. She tries to memorize the directions—not complicated, basically three right turns. On these roads, Hannah can peg this beast at eighty plus and get there in no time.

Sloane fades in and out. Hannah checks her breathing.

"Hey." She gives Sloane a light tap to the face. "No. Stay with me, dammit."

A notice pops up on the screen of her phone. It's from the site.

A new live stream has just begun.

Hannah tries hard to keep one eye on the road and one on her phone. Much like the other live stream, the camera bounces and jiggles, blurs and then clears. She can see the snap into place that she now knows all too well. The phone is being placed in a harness on someone's chest.

The username is new, yet familiar.

THE_Zach_Winter.

She recognizes what's on the screen. It's a neighborhood.

Hannah holds her breath. This can't be happening. He's on Corny's street. The camera is walking down the street toward her sister's house.

"No. No!"

She turns up the volume on the phone. Looks up. Makes a hard right turn. The tires scream. She pushes the gas to the floor.

Is that really Zach?

What the hell is he doing?

He's only a few doors down from Corny's house. From Luna. Hannah's ears thump with her pounding heart. She screams at her phone, begging the screen to stop. Never felt more helpless in her life.

"This was always the plan, Hannah," Zach says.

Hannah peels away from the universe. Knuckles turn white as she grips the wheel.

"Saw how you looked every morning. Your eyes, the way they lit up when you talked about little Luna." Zach's voice is so sweet and warm. So chilling at the same time. "You talked about her all the time. Like she was your own. You wanted it to be true, but it wasn't."

"Stop. Just stop."

Her eyes are full, frantic mind fumbling for solutions that are not coming.

"They don't deserve her. You do."

"Zach, please!"

"*We* deserve this, Hannah."

Through the fog of her tears, her vibrating emotions, she sees the emergency clinic up ahead. She looks to Sloane. She's not moving, her head against the window. With one eye on the phone's screen, she sees that Zach has stopped. He's standing in the shade across from Corny's house.

Hannah's brain burns. *Think. Do something.*

The view turns slightly to the driveway. A silver sedan pulls out. Jake's car.

"Oh my God."

He was waiting for Jake to leave. Zach either didn't want to take on the husband, or the act of killing is losing its charm. That doesn't seem like the case. Nothing makes sense.

The next view on the screen turns Hannah's blood ice cold.

Corny is holding Luna's hand as they stand on the front porch. They wave as Jake drives down the street. Hannah can hear Zach breathe harder, excitement circulating in and out of his lungs. Corny and Luna go back into the house.

Zach moves forward.

"No!"

Hannah swipes away the site, taps Corny's number.

It rings once... twice... three times.

"Come on... come on." Hannah taps speaker, then pulls the site back up. Eyes go back and forth between the screen and the road.

Zach is crossing the street, only a few steps from the front yard.

"Answer the fucking phone!"

"Hannah?" Corny says.

"Lock the door. Get Luna and go upstairs. Call 9-1-1. Hide—"

"What? What are you—"

"Listen to me! That coffee shop guy who killed those people is outside your house."

"What..." Corny's voice trails off.

"Please just do what I said. Get Luna. Find a weapon and hide."

"Luna, come with mommy." Hannah can hear the deadbolt click.

"Call 9-1-1." Hannah's mind rolls. She looks to the back of her phone. "I'm calling someone else to come there now."

"Hannah—"

"I know. I'm scared too but you gotta be strong for that little girl."

"I know but—"

"Courtney. Remember Mom's boyfriends? This isn't any different."

Hannah hears movement on the other end of the phone. She can hear the confused, sweet voice of Luna.

"What's happening, Mommy? Where are we going?"

Hannah's heart breaks into a million pieces.

She slams on the brakes. Swerves. Shaken, she realizes she hasn't looked at the road in who knows how long. Lost track of anything resembling time. The emergency clinic is just up ahead.

"Okay, we're going upstairs." Hannah can tell she's half-talking to her and half to Luna. "I've got you."

"Courtney, tell Luna I love—"

The call ends. Hannah punches the gas, covers the remaining distance and screeches to a stop in front of the clinic. She looks to her phone. The view is Zach checking the door.

"You piece of shit."

She removes Detective Huston's business card from the back of her phone. It's a long shot but she needs everyone and everything right now. It rings multiple times, then reaches the front desk.

A man on the other end starts to speak. Hannah cuts him off.

"This is Hannah Rush. Yes, that Hannah Rush. I need Detective Huston and everyone in that fucking building to go to my sister's house."

"Ma'am. I need you to please slow down and—"

"Zach Winter is there. He is about to go inside. My sister is there with her daughter."

There's a pause and she can hear the man cover the phone. A muffled conversation.

"What's the address, Hannah?" Detective Huston asks.

Hannah yells the address. Repeats it. Pleads for him to hurry.

"We will," he says. "Where are you?"

"Never mind. I'll tell you everything later. Just help my family."

"I will."

Hannah hangs up. Goes back to the site. Zach has a crowbar at the back door.

"No. No. No."

She looks over to Sloane. She isn't breathing. Hannah flies out, racing around the front of the truck. Throwing open the door, she pulls Sloane out and muscles her toward the clinic.

Hannah's imagination screams, ripping through thoughts of what the phone screen is showing right now as it's stuffed in her back pocket. As the electronic door slides open, two nurses race out to meet her. They take Sloane from her.

"What happened?" one asks.

"Fight. She's been beaten. Maybe stabbed or shot." Hannah hands her over, pulling her phone from her pocket. "She's a friend of mine. She had a pulse but she's stopped breathing."

The nurses disappear into the back of the clinic with Sloane.

Hannah stares into the screen of the phone, holding it with both hands while pacing in the lobby of the clinic.

Zach is inside the house.

The comments roll below the live stream like a waterfall. Hannah ignores them all.

Zach has a large tactical blade in his hand. The blade catches the lights overhead. The same one he had in the video that night he said he committed murder for Hannah.

Now he says he's doing this for her too.

Hannah watches. Helpless. Breathless.

Another nurse tries to talk to her. She sees her lips move, but she doesn't hear the words. Pulling away from the nurse's outstretched hands, she moves quick to the other end of the lobby, clutching the phone tight.

Zach is walking up the stairs.

Hannah's hands tremble. The screen bounces. At the bottom of the screen, there's the option to join with video. She has to buy some time for someone to get there.

"Almost, Hannah. Don't be scared." Zach is almost at the top of the stairs.

Hannah's face appears on the screen, live streaming from the clinic lobby.

"Zach. Stop. Don't do this."

Patients in the lobby turn to watch.

There's a pause. She can see that Zach has stopped a few steps from the second floor. Must have noticed the live stream.

"Hannah?"

Hannah talks directly into the camera. "Yes. It's me. Zach, please do not do this. Just walk out of the house."

"I can't. Too late. This was the plan all along."

He starts moving up the stairs again.

"Zach—"

"You don't see it. How could you? But all this was always for you."

He's reached the top of the stairs. The camera turns as if he's looking down the hall. Toward the bedrooms.

"Stop! Do not do this, Zach!" Tears flood. Hannah is screaming. "I will never talk to you again. Do you fucking hear me!"

Several nurses circle, surrounding her.

Zach stops, turns slightly. Something has caught his attention.

"Did you call the cops?"

Hannah doesn't answer. He must hear something outside the house.

The image jerks as Zach moves faster. He checks the bathroom. Rips the shower curtain back. Hannah begs and pleads with him to listen to her. Anything to buy precious seconds. Zach is raging. Throwing open doors left and right. Everything stops.

The camera levels on the bed in Corny's room.

Hannah falls to her knees.

No... no... no. Corny hid under the bed. Like when they were kids.

Zach drops down. The screen goes black, only slight cracks of light coming through while his chest is pressed so close to the floor. Hannah covers her mouth.

The screen jumps back up and Zach continues his search. "I can't believe you're doing this!"

Hannah can hear the fury in Zach's voice.

Nurses try to help Hannah up to her feet. She swats them away, eyes locked on the screen. Hoping, praying the police get there in time.

Zach stops at a closet door. He tries the knob.

It's being held shut.

They're inside.

Zach doesn't hesitate to jam the crowbar in. He yanks and pulls a like a madman. The wood cracks and splinters. Screams and cries sound from inside the closet.

The door flings open.

Huddled on the floor is her sister, her arms wrapped tight around Luna. Even through the screen, Hannah can see the terror in Luna's eyes.

Hannah's heart stops beating. The world tilts.

"Zach!"

"I love you, Hannah, no matter what."

Onscreen, the knife pulls back out of view.

Hannah's throat shreds as she releases an inhuman cry.

THIRTY

ONE WEEK LATER

Hannah walks in the park alone.

The air is cool but not cold.

Shafts of light warm her face as she passes from the shade into the heat of the sun. Her hands push deep into the pocket of her charcoal-gray hoodie. She likes to keep her face covered as much as possible. At least for now.

Her story is still fresh on the minds of millions.

Her face and body still ache. Teeth still grind when she sleeps. But the visible wounds have begun the later stages of healing. Bruises shades of purple and graying pinks. Cuts and scrapes coming together and will disappear soon.

The wounds inside of her may never close, let alone heal.

Most nights she wakes up in a cold sweat. Haunting thoughts jar her awake. Screaming. Shaking. Nightmares of what might have happened a week ago.

What might have happened if they hadn't arrived in time.

If the police, led by Detectives Huston and Rebar, hadn't gotten to Corny's house when they did. If they hadn't stopped Zach as he stood in the closet doorway, that blade drawn back in his hand.

Hannah has no way of knowing how far Zach was willing to go.

Would he have killed Corny?

She constantly wrestles with it in her mind. Always fighting the spiral. The spinning down into the dark depths of her own imagination. Heart-wrenching visions of what might have happened.

Her phone buzzes. A text from Corny lights the screen.

Just landed.

Hannah smiles—the first smile in days. Corny, Jake, and Luna are taking a much-needed escape to Hawaii. Hannah exhales. Didn't realize she was holding her breath.

The damage that day did to Luna is hard to measure.

Corny had held her tight on the floor of that closet. Done her best to shield Luna from the sights and sounds of everything that happened. The adults tell themselves it will all be okay with time. But the concerns are real. Kids are such perceptive sponges there's little chance Luna will walk away from that day without her own emotional cuts and bruises.

Zach had lunged at Huston and Rebar. They had not hesitated to put him down.

How much Luna saw is unknown. No matter how much Corny tried to cover Luna's eyes and ears, there's no way the gunshots didn't rattle her to her little core.

It's early days, but Luna has at least been open to talking to someone about it all. A good sign. She's young. There's time to heal a lot of things. Everyone hopes what the therapist says is true. That kids are truly as resilient as rumored.

Another text from Corny.

See u here soon?

Hannah thinks, then taps out a truthful, noncommittal response.

We'll see how things go. Glad ur safe. Hug Luna for me.

Pocketing her phone, Hannah does a quick scan of the area. Looks over the faces. All the men, women, and children going about their normal daily lives.

Normal looks nice. Boring seems exciting.

Hannah's hard eyes skip over each one of them, searching for the one person in the passing crowd she seeks. Someone she hasn't seen in quite some time.

Her father sits at a gray cement picnic table near a creek.

A nice spot in the shade. Soft sounds of children playing nearby. The park's treehouse just over his shoulder. Parents push strollers past him. Joggers. Dog walkers. Public, yet private at the same time.

Right where Hannah asked Corny to tell him to meet her.

Looking him over, so unsure of what to do, she considers turning and running. Hate balls up inside of her. She can taste it rising to the back of her throat. Can feel the gun tucked behind her back calling out to her. Begging to come out and offer a final solution to her problems.

Her father turns.

As he sees her, he begins to stand.

Hannah holds up her hand. Flat, like a stop

sign, telling him to stay where he is. He takes the not-so-subtle hint, planting his feet exactly as she says. Hard for Hannah to tell what's going on behind those steel-gray eyes of his.

Must always assume the worst with this man.

Pulling the envelope from her back pocket, she waves it as she gets within a few feet of him. She sees no need to delay this meeting with small talk or unneeded, unwanted chitchat.

"Not sure how much is in here," she says, "but I'm not an idiot. I'm taking your money."

He smiles. "Always been a smart little girl. It's a goodly sum."

She brushes off *little girl*.

"Not completely sure what you're trying to buy with this." Runs her fingers around the edges of the envelope, as she has ever since Corny gave it to her. Avoids eye contact. "Obviously you're trying to buy me. Buy Corny. Mom. Maybe buy forgiveness from all of us. I don't know." Looks up with the hardest of stares. "You can't afford any of those big-ticket items. You know that, right?"

"Pretty sure you know my character traits and—"

"No. Not sure I know much about you at all. Other than the obvious."

"Which is?"

"You're a complete piece of shit."

"Oh. That." He resets. "What I meant was, what I was going to say, is that *buying forgiveness* thing, that's not what I'm about. I'm buying something else. Something for myself."

"And that is..."

"Purchasing as much peace of mind as I can."

"Sounds expensive."

"Very."

Hannah remembers that movie. The one with the guy who could figure out what the contents of the envelope were without opening it. He'd figure it out by asking the right questions.

"Let's see if I can guess what peace costs a mind like yours."

He nods, enjoying the game between them.

"So, given your ego, it's a big check. You'd want to impress me."

He shrugs, a smug smile forms.

"Think I saw recently where you had a plan with some guy. Seemed pretty sweet. What was his name..." Fakes trying to remember. Snaps her fingers. "Alex Nord. Looked like you two had this big true-crime entertainment package in the works. Sound about right?"

All the smugness drains from her father's face.

Hannah shrugs, matching the slick vibe he's been firing at her.

"You really going to pretend you don't know anything about any of that?" She holds up her phone. Shows him the missed calls from the unknown 512 number. Unknown until now. "You've been calling me, haven't you? This number just happened to pop up that first night. Odd."

He doesn't answer, has shut down. No longer enjoying the game. He's morphed into an expressionless man on trial offering up nothing to the prosecution.

"I saw the same number in some other places too. But the place that really caught my eye was one I found about a week ago. In Oklahoma." Hannah watches his eyes go dead. "It was buried deep. Still, that's some sloppy work using that number—"

She takes a beat, savoring the moment.

"I had to have an incredibly boring, painful dinner with an IT guy from where I used to work. One who's been trying to sleep with your daughter for a while. Regardless, he helped me crack open this laptop—one I got in Oklahoma.

All kinds of cool, super-fun shit in there. And if memory serves, that phone number was listed in some really hard-to-find files." He may not be enjoying the game anymore, but she is. "Any of that ringing true? Help me out. I'm not very smart. It's all fuzzy."

"Not sure I understand what you think you know, Hannah." He squints, looking at the phone's screen. "That number doesn't look familiar. Who memorizes phone numbers these days?"

Hannah's blood starts to simmer. "This playtime for you?"

"Hannah."

He tries to touch her shoulder. She pulls away quick. Takes everything she has not to pull her gun and turn his skull to mist.

"Okay." He takes a step back. "You've been through a lot. I saw it all on the news. It's horrible what's happened." He shrugs. "Sounds like one hell of a story. Can't wait to hear more about it. Hope you'll tell it to me one day after you've had some time to heal."

"Not sure the story's over."

His expression alters ever so slightly. That got his attention. Hannah knows this is as close as she might get to making him nervous.

"What do you mean by that?"

"By what, Father?"

"The ending."

"Back to this." Hannah shakes the envelope, returning to her questions about the contents. "It would need to be an impressive amount, but also one that would have a purpose. Given what you've done, you'd want me to have enough to go away on, right? Maybe you gave it to Corny as a way for me to escape what was coming. That your way of being a *good dad*, Father?"

"Hannah, I don't—"

"Can't be completely sure, I'm only a *little girl*, but it seems that Alex Nord was paid to write a book about some psycho named Logan Burke, as well as a group of crazy followers of his. Again, it's all fuzzy, but something about a hard-to-find, dark corner of the internet. Crazy men killing in the name of women who don't give a damn about them. Looks like it happened more than once." Hannah levels her eyes on him. "The whole thing is nutty as hell. But there's this company—one that bought out Nord and his previous book deal. It's a new company, and oddly enough, it was given some seed money by another firm."

"Interesting stuff."

"Isn't it? There's that, but there's also that

through this winding maze of shell companies and other MBA, CFA, blah-blah, this new company not only paid Nord to write the book, but also had deals in place with a rather large streaming service. Some licensing deals for podcasts and all kinds of stuff. Too much for me to truly understand, but some pretty eye-popping money on the line. Wait." She holds her hand out as if an idea just landed from above. "You're a big-brained venture capital guy, right? You're deep into all that stuff. Any of that sound familiar at all?"

He doesn't even attempt to respond.

"Last thing, before I tell you to truly *fuck off*." Hannah locks into his eyes. "This web of companies and bank accounts? They also poured money into a rogue little company in Oklahoma that houses the websites that no sane, legitimate organization wants to be part of. Seems to me that it's encouraging the crazy. Maybe an incubator of sorts. Place to hatch new true-crime franchise media ideas. All so it can create and bundle up content to sell to the very public it threatens to harm."

"How much?" her father asks.

"How much for what?"

"For these wild theories to stop before things

get out of hand."

"Wow. Now that's interesting." Hannah stops. Waits for a family to pass by. Looks up to the sky. "What's even more interesting is you sent someone to follow me. A rather large man came to my apartment, followed me, and unfortunately died trying to protect us."

Her father keeps his face as a void.

"He recognized Nord, so you must have shown him pictures of me and Nord at some point. Protect your investments, maybe?" Hannah feels her knuckles crack as she balls up her fists inside the hoodie pocket. "Guessing Nord let you know he made contact with me. Right?"

"Again, I have no idea—"

"That what passes for love and caring with you? Realizing that you unleashed the dogs on your daughter so you send a hired gun to protect her? Did you know Zach was on that board? Did you help push him my way?" She shakes the envelope one last time. "Is this money really for me to run away and hide on? You knew what was coming for me, so you tried to make it look good. Make it seem like you were trying to pay back your sins. Make good with the family you left behind."

Silence from her father. Emotionless. Vacant.

The wind blows. Dogs bark. Kids play in the background.

A quiet pause that seems to stretch on forever.

Hannah assassinates the silence.

"This is it, man. This is your last chance to tell me the truth. Because when I leave this park, we are done. There will be no communication with me. Nothing with Courtney and certainly not one fucking word with Luna. You get me?"

"Hannah, listen to me. You've been through a lot. But let's try and—"

"That your answer? You want to stick with that?"

He holds out his hands, doing his best to fade any responsibility.

Hannah holds her stare. Studying. Reading. She may not know all the answers to what happened, but she can see the broad strokes. Probably deeper and darker than she even realizes. But what she does know without a doubt is what her father has always been. What he will always be.

A monster.

She opens the envelope and eyes the check. Raises her eyebrows. Presses her lips together with a tight nod. "That is a lot of money." Pockets the check. "Still not enough."

Turning her back on him, she walks away. Puts as much distance between them as she can, moving out and into the rest of the park. A small part of her hopes he'll call for her to stop. That he'll talk to her, come clean. Offer the truth as a form of cleansing.

He doesn't.

Hannah breathes in and out, pushing back the flooding emotions. She hears a voice in the back of her mind calling out through the angry fog. It's her own voice this time, not Corny.

This isn't good or bad, it just simply is.

Now, go find some fun in the precious moments after the horrible shit.

HANNAH DROPS her bag on the filthy bed of the cheap roadside motel off Highway 87.

Same one that she, Nord, and Sloane hung out in a little over a week ago. Still stinks of mildew and desperation.

She lays out the laptop, hard drives, thumb drive, multiple smartphones, and everything else she collected from the barn in Oklahoma.

Including Nord's bag that was still in Sloane's truck. Hannah had managed to stash it all before the police came raining down on her at the clinic.

Once she saw the detectives rush in and knew that Corny and Luna were safe, she'd surprised herself. She'd pushed free from the nurses and raced out to the truck, knowing that it was only a matter of time before the police tracked her down.

She found a cheap motel much like this one not far from the clinic, then hid the bag in the ceiling. The cheap tile was easy to push up and slide the bag into.

Not perfect, but she couldn't run the risk of the police impounding the truck and taking the contents. Hannah knew whatever was in that bag held the answers she and Sloane had fought so damn hard for.

Sloane was released from the hospital a couple of days ago.

Hannah left her alone but kept constant tabs on her condition. The media has been all over her as well. The hospital did a decent job of keeping them at bay. Good thing Sloane knows how to go ghost. She only hopes she learned enough from Sloane to pull that off as well.

She places bright, neon-yellow Post-it notes on the lid of the laptop and the phones.

She didn't lie to her father. She did have dinner with that annoying IT guy Neil. Talked sweet and nice to him. He was happy to help. *Happy to do anything to help her.* And why not? Hannah is more damaged now than ever. Even more for him to fix, marry, and manage. Hannah leaned into his ego and dull desires, all while talking him into cracking open the passcode-protected laptops and various other tech.

Surprisingly, it didn't take long. He is a smart dude.

IT Neil carved through the security like it wasn't even there. Hannah thanked him, gave him a kiss on the cheek, and told him that she'd call him.

She won't.

In the bathroom sits the remains of the hair dye she worked through her hair not long ago. Picked up some fake glasses and was able get some colored contacts to make her eyes brown. Not sure it's enough, but it should at least keep the media hounds off her at first glance. Even added some fake tattoos to her arms and neck.

She checks the time.

With a sharpie, she writes the login information on the Post-it note that she stuck to the laptop. Does the same to the phones, then arranges them in a nice, neat line. Under them, she lays out the contents of Nord's bag. All the notes, files, and a half-completed manuscript. From her go-bag she pulls a healthy stack of twenties and a dozen or so pre-paid Visa cards, laying them next to the laptop. A little something to fill in the gaps during the journey.

She looks to the time.

She'll be here soon.

Hannah's flight to Hawaii leaves in a few hours. She can't wait to see them.

Hannah had deposited the check from her father immediately after she left him in the park. There was an ATM across the street.

She didn't want to give him a chance to cancel or put a hold on the funds. It was a lot of money—not crazy money, but enough for someone like Hannah to call it quits for a long while—and Hannah felt a pang of guilt for taking it. Some might consider it wrong, but Hannah considered it hers. Payment earned.

The money won't buy what her father wants, however. Peace of mind was never up for sale. Besides, Hannah will make things right in a different sort of way.

There's a knock at the door.

Hannah runs her finger across the top of the last Post-it.

Opening the door, she sees Sloane standing with one hand on her hip holster. Always on alert this one. Hannah can't help but smile.

Sloane does not.

She looks better than the last time she was with her. She's breathing, for one, but human-like color has also returned to her face. The fight in her eyes is back as well.

Hannah snuffs out the urge to hug her.

"It's all there." Hannah thumbs back toward the bed. "Do whatever you want with it. Hunt down all of them or leave them alone. Lady's choice."

Sloane's cold eyes take in the buffet of information in front of her. She steps into the room, checking the corners, eye to the bathroom, then stands over the bed. The answers to everything she's been tracking, hunting ever since Logan Burke robbed her of her life, is here.

Even Sloane can't fight a smile. A slight one, but it's there.

She turns to say something. Maybe a thanks.

Like a ghost, Hannah is gone.

ACKNOWLEDGMENTS

I say the same thing with each book and will continue saying it until it stops being true... you can't do a damn thing alone. So, I'd like to thank the people who gave help and hope during this fun and occasionally nutty writing life.

The list of those people is insanely long. Multiplies by the day actually. And I love them all dearly, so the thought of leaving someone out and listening to them whine and complain later is a little more than I can take on right now.

Fine. I'll point out a couple.

A big thanks to my longtime editor and keeper of the faith, Elizabeth A. White and Christie Hartman for that much needed final look.

Many thanks to the great writers that I'm honored to call friends. You've saved me from giving up on more than one occasion, and without question, I have taken far more than I have given. Hopefully, you know who you are.

Per usual, I can't do any of this without my

roommates. Also known as my amazing family. Words don't cover it.

And finally.

If you're reading this right now, you deserve the biggest thank you of all. Even if we've never met, you've been cool and kind enough to grab a copy of my book and give it a read. That there, my dear, friendly, gorgeous reader deserves one big-ass ACKNOWLEDGEMENT.

Thanks, good people.

If you keep reading. I'll keep writing.

Deal?

ABOUT THE AUTHOR

Mike has been a waiter, securities trader, dishwasher, investment manager, and an unpaid Hollywood intern. He's quit corporate America, come back, been fired, been promoted, been fired, and currently he writes stories about questionable people making questionable decisions.

Keep up with Mike at...
www.mikemccrary.com
mccrarynews@mikemccrary.com